Awake As A Stranger

AWAKENING

Part One

D1082242

By
Diane M. Dresback

This is a work of fiction. Names, characters, places, and incidents either are the product of the author's imagination or are used fictitiously, and resemblance to actual persons, living or dead, business establishments, events, or locales is entirely coincidental.

Published by Mindclover Productions LLC

Copyright © 2021 by Diane M. Dresback

All rights reserved. This book, or parts thereof, may not be reproduced in any form without permission.

DEDICATION

My Awake As A Stranger trilogy is dedicated to you who I will probably never know nor walk in your shoes—Your lives and stories are meaningful and valuable even if misunderstood.

ACKNOWLEDGEMENTS

Rick Silber for loving me and my purple chair.

Trenton Greyoak and Devon Dresback for listening to my ideas and continuing to encourage me in my varied creative endeavors.

Michael Hilton and Trenton Greyoak for discussing the Awake As A Stranger trilogy story in depth as it developed.

The North Texas Writers MeetUp group for invaluable feedback during the part of my writing process that I lived in Texas.

Deanna and Trenton Greyoak for cover design.

Teresa Young for delineating discrepancies in my characters and my story.

My parents who are no longer with me (Charles and Mildred Gerg, and Terri Cox). I hope somehow they know and approve of my stories.

1

TREAZ

Treaz stood before the bathroom mirror gawking at her naked body. It was not because she was vain or had poor body image but because the person reflecting back was not her. It was the body of a stranger.

She cupped her cheeks, unable to look away. Who was this woman? Brushing back straight, fine, red hair revealed deep green eyes and pale skin packed with freckles. The woman stood tall, and was a most unhealthy skinny. Where had the real Treaz gone?

"What's going on?" She said aloud, surprised at her high pitched voice.

Treaz reached out to touch the glass to ensure it was an actual reflection. Her fingers glided against the cool, smooth surface. Had she actually woken up? She did feel exceptionally groggy, like a fog surrounded her. Her vision blurry.

A few moments ago, as she forced her heavy eyelids open, she felt different. Something seemed way off, yet she couldn't place it. A shiver enveloped her unclothed body because she never slept without pajamas, and she had awoken without a stitch on.

She blinked and blinked again trying to make sense of what she saw—a woman at least ten years younger. Had she somehow traveled back in time? No. It must be some weird, lucid dream giving every indication it was real. This was bizarre. Treaz splashed her face with cold water and swallowed sips from the faucet.

Reentering the bedroom, she hunted for and engaged a light switch causing a dull illumination to confirm what she already had discovered in the bathroom—she was not in her own house. The mattress lay on the floor, no box springs. Above the bed hung two kitten posters. Piles of clothes were thrown everywhere. Maybe this was a kind of out-of-body experience?

A wave of mental exhaustion hit. Her eyes ached. It was too much—too confusing. Treaz turned extinguished the light and crawled back in the bed, yanking the covers over her head. The sheets put off a funky odor. She liked clean sheets, not ones that hadn't been laundered in a month. Can you smell in a dream?

She recounted the night before had been her thirty-second birthday. She vaguely remembered polishing off several vodka concoctions and most of a bottle of wine all on her own. With the after-effects of too much alcohol evident by the hammering in her skull, she massaged her temples. Curling her knees up to her chest, she shut her eyes willing herself to sleep so she could truly wake up. Wait until Grammie hears about this wild dream!

Later, Treaz rolled stiffly from her stomach to her back—still naked. She opened her eyes to light streaming in from two broken blinds on the window. This was not her room! Stretching out her long sallow arms, she studied the abundance of freckles. How can this be? What was going on? Tears filled her eyes as she buried her face in her hands. She was losing her grip on reality. She was having a breakdown, just like her mother had suffered.

"No!" She told herself firmly. There must be a logical explanation.

Nothing resembled her own clothes, so she wrapped the blanket around her shoulders and peeked out the bedroom door to see if anyone else might be there—sharing her crazy hallucination.

No one else materialized in the apartment, consisting of a small kitchen and a living room area with modest furnishings. Unwashed dishes stacked high in the sink, bread crumbs and hardened beads of strawberry jelly dotted the counter, and cat knick-knacks adorned most flat surfaces. On the wobbly kitchen table was a cereal bowl holding pinkish curdled milk and an unopened nine-inch-square cardboard box with nothing written on the outside to indicate its contents.

A thirty-inch television was on a stand next to a stack of *People* magazines, and a candy dish containing red and silver foiled chocolate kisses. On the bookshelf in the corner sat a gaudy plastic cat whose eyes shifted mechanically back and forth with a faint ticking indicating each passing second. Held in its paws, a display of the current time and date, 6:13 am, December 18, 2016. Treaz frowned. December 18th? Three days after her birthday. How had three full days disappeared? Did she die and reincarnate?

A wave of dizziness and disorientation hit her. Bile rose in her throat. She dashed to the bathroom, closed her eyes to avoid acknowledging her proximity to the nasty toilet bowl, and retched nothing but the water she sipped earlier. After tugging herself back up, she caught sight of those green eyes staring back at her in the mirror, boring a hole into her psyche.

Her heart thumped. Treaz took a bed sheet and draped it over the vanity light fixture hiding the mirror, not wanting to be reminded of who she was, or rather, who she wasn't.

There must be someone who could help make sense of what made no sense to her.   She ran from the apartment into the hallway, which appeared abandoned with the long stretch of doors. Treaz rushed to the one across the hall and began banging. "Hello? Hello? Can you help me?"

The door cracked opened and a woman peered out. Upon seeing Treaz, she widened the door further.

"What's my name?" blurted out Treaz, perspiration beading on her brow.

"Uh. I don't know."

"Please, who am I?"

The lady stared at her, taking in her blanket draped body and disheveled appearance.

"You don't know my name?"

"No. I only see you going in and out of your apartment."

Treaz opened her mouth. The woman recognized her.

"Sorry, I gotta go," said the neighbor closing the door.

Treaz pounded again, "No, please! I need help. I don't know how I got here."

The woman called from behind the door, "I'm gonna call security if you don't stop." The pounding and pleas continued. "I'm calling security."

Treaz collapsed against the wall, sliding down to the cold cement, her mind a flurry of confusion. Maybe this is really me and the other life was a dream. But no, no—she pictured Grammie and the house they had shared so clearly. That couldn't all have been a dream. She wept. *I AM becoming my mother.*

A middle-aged man wearing a uniform squatted in front of Treaz. His voice gentle. "Miss Edwards?" No response. "Miss Edwards. Are you alright?"

She frowned and looked into his eyes, her face streaked with tears.

"Danielle. What's going on?"

Danielle Edwards? She shook her head. "My name is Treaz."

4

He put his hand on her shoulder. "You flipping out on something?"

"No. My name's Treaz Popa." She grasped his arm. "What am I doing here?"

"You live here."

She started crying again.

The security guard attempted to help her up. "Look, let's move you back in your apart—"

She pushed him away. "I don't live in there. Don't make me go back."

"Do you want me to call somebody?"

Treaz pointed at her body. "Who is this?"

His eyebrows arched. "Yeah. I think I need to find some help." He stepped away—too far for Treaz to hear his phone conversation, but close enough for him to keep a wary eye on her. As sirens grew louder, she covered her face with the blanket trying to ignore her living nightmare.

More footsteps approached and she heard the guard say, "Danielle Edwards. She's really freaked out."

"Miss Edwards?" came a deep female voice. "Danielle? Can you uncover your face?"

Slowly, she lowered the blanket for the EMT.

"My name is not Danielle, it's Treaz," she said in a raspy voice.

"Okay, Treaz. My name is Candace. And my partner is Brent."

Treaz quickly glanced at Brent, then back to the woman.

"Do you know where you are?" asked Candace.

She shook her head.

Brent addressed the guard who stood nearby. "You say she lives here?"

He nodded at the open apartment door behind them.

5

"That's not my house. I'm not going back in there," Treaz said in a loud, stern voice.

"Alright. We won't force you," said Candace. Then she turned to the security officer. "Can you find her something to wear?"

After a few minutes, he returned with some clothes and handed them to Candace.

Treaz tightened the blanket. "I don't want to wear those. They're not mine."

"You don't want to be naked, do you? Let's stand you up."

Candace and Brent raised her to her feet. Treaz allowed them to help her put on the stranger's clothing. They fit loosely over the rail-thin body.

"We're going to take you to get checked out," reassured Candace.

Perhaps these people could help her return to her real life—her real body.

Candace gripped Treaz's arm. "Can you walk?"

With an emergency tech supporting each side, Treaz shuffled down the stairs to the awaiting ambulance. She squinted at the brilliant blue sky, not expecting such glare for the forecasted tropical depression from the gulf. There was no rain, nor puddles. Instead she was surrounded by a simple landscape of beige rock, a ground cover of orange and gold flowers, and a periodic cactus. The blood drained from her face. "I'm not in San Antonio?"

"Nope. Phoenix, Arizona. Home to two hundred ninety-nine days of sunshine a year," said Brent.

"How'd I get here?"

Candace opened the back doors of the ambulance. "We're taking you somewhere to find that out."

Treaz hesitated before climbing in, but she complied knowing that she certainly couldn't cope with this by herself. She almost bumped her head on the roof, being much taller than she was

6

used to. Once inside, she realized something was missing. "My bracelet," she shouted in a panic, grasping her wrist. "Someone stole my bracelet." Her head jerked up as a chill shot down her spine. A figure flashed in her mind—a man outside her bedroom window that last night at her home. Had he taken her bracelet? Had he stolen her body? Everything felt like a dream. If she could just rouse herself. Treaz pinched her arms hard.

Candace grabbed her hands. "Danielle, stop pinching yourself."

"I'm not Danielle! I need to wake up." She struggled to free her hands. A sharp jab went into her arm and she whimpered.

"Just relax," said Candace.

Soon her body lost its tension, and the EMT's laid her on the gurney placing a restraining belt across her torso. Her thoughts turned to her grandmother. She experienced a horrific sense of doubt that she would ever see her alive again. That inextricably painful thought brought stinging to her eyes. Would Grammie and Treaz both die alone?

2

TREAZ

The glass doors of Caring Hearts Hospital Emergency Room glided open as Treaz's gurney pushed down a white hallway past scurrying nurses and worried family members. They came to a halt inside a light blue colored room where a young, upbeat woman dressed in purple scrubs stood in the corner watching. The emergency technicians transferred Treaz from the gurney to a hospital bed.

Candace patted Treaz's hand. "Good luck to you," and exited with Brent.

"Hello Danielle. I'm Jennifer," said the woman in the scrubs as she rolled a stand holding a laptop on it to the side of the bed.

Still tired from the sedation, Treaz shook her head. "Please, call me Treaz. My name is Treaz."

Jennifer nodded, giving no indication the request posed a problem. "Okay, Treaz. I have a few questions for you before the nurse gets here. Do you have someone we should call?"

"Grammie."

"Your grandmother?"

Treaz nodded.

Jennifer typed some information and looked up. "Great. What's her number?"

Rubbing her face with her hands, Treaz shrugged. "I don't know." How could she not know her best friend's phone number? Was it wrong to claim your Grammie as your best friend?

Images of her grandmother's corpse alone in the nursing home riled her up. "This stupid Danielle woman took my body!"

Jennifer seemed taken back and tried to calm Treaz. "It's okay. Let me see if I can give you some water." She made a phone call, talking quietly into the receiver for an extended period.

"It's only water," said Treaz, irritated.

"Thank you," Jennifer said before hanging up and turning to Treaz. "I know. But we just have to get permission from the nurse. Someone will bring it soon. Let's see if we can get through some of this other information." She consulted her screen. "I know you like to be called, Treaz. But what is your legal name?"

"Nadia Popa."

The woman looked at her. "It isn't Danielle Edwards?"

How many times did she need to tell people? Especially this pollyanna girl. "I don't know this Danielle woman."

"Sure. What's your address and phone number?"

Treaz shrugged.

"I just thought…" Jennifer stopped. "Do you remember your birthday?"

That was a question Treaz could answer. "December 15th."

"How old are you?"

"I'm thirty-two."

Jennifer glanced up, smiling. "Well congratulations. You just had a birthday and you look fantastic for your age."

Treaz recalled a few days before, running into a previous coworker while at the grocery store. Honestly, she barely could think of her name—Lori or Lucy? Yes, Lucy. After receiving what she assumed to be an obligatory invitation to a Christmas party at Lucy's home, Treaz declined. She avoided much interaction with Lucy, thinking of her as just a popular rich kid who hadn't worked for anything she owned. How can a twenty-two year old afford a BMW?

"That's my birthday. I'm sure I'll be busy," Treaz had said knowing her 'busy' would involve a visit to see Grammie before going home to spend the evening alone.

"We can celebrate your birthday as well," Lucy said with a grin.

Might she have gone to Lucy's place? That made no sense.

"Have you consumed any alcohol or taken any drugs recently?" asked Jennifer.

"I did drink some that first night," Treaz admitted, remembering she'd celebrated her birthday by herself, which entailed drinking alone, something she rarely did. "But that has nothing to do with this. I haven't had anything since, and I don't take drugs."

Jennifer's voice droned on. "Do you have insurance?"

Treaz looked down at her long legs realizing she was answering questions as if she was in her own body. "I don't know."

"Do you have any allergies?"

"I don't know."

"Are you taking any prescription medica—"

"Jennifer," said Treaz coldly, her head pounding and body feeling disjointed. "What do you think?"

The young woman stared at Treaz for a moment, then nodded. "We'll just wait for the nurse, then." She pushed the computer cart a few feet away and continued typing on the keyboard while watching Treaz out of the corner of her eye.

Treaz fought to register her present predicament. Maybe the vodka had been tainted. Perhaps Grammie had brought on an old Romanian curse. She had told tales of mysterious exploits while growing up in Romania, and she did say cryptic things quite often, especially as she got older. Could this be an old world rite of passage? Like, you turn thirty-two and bam: you're suddenly transformed to live someone else's life. Of course, that made absolutely no sense either.

A woman of about forty-five with no makeup and hair pulled tight into a bun, entered the room carrying a tiny cup of water. Jennifer hurried to exit. Treaz swallowed down the one ounce serving and asked for more.

"Sorry, that's it for now."

Treaz shoved the empty cup back at the woman.

"My name's Stacy. I'm one of the resident counselors here." She repositioned the mobile computer stand back by the side of the bed. "Why don't you tell me what brings you in today."

"Well," Treaz hesitated, struggling about where to start.

"Just tell me what's going on."

Treaz exhaled. "This morning, I woke up in someone else's body. A woman named Danielle Edwards. I'm a thousand miles from my home in San Antonio and I don't know how I got here. I think it might be because of a guy who was outside my home. And I've lost three days." She stopped, waiting for Stacy's shocked reaction, but the woman focused on making notes on the laptop.

"You say you are in the body of someone else?"

Treaz nodded.

More clicking of the keys. "And you have no recollection of how you got to Phoenix?"

"No clue. I'm the same me on the inside, but on the outside, I'm this Danielle woman. It sounds crazy which, I guess, is why I'm here. I need a possible answer."

12

Stacy stopped typing. "I'm not certain I can give you that answer, but we could spend some time talking. Danielle, have you —"

"Please, call me Treaz. That's my real name; well my nickname."

Stacy nodded. "Why don't you start with what happened before you woke up this morning."

"I was at my Grammie's nursing home." She exhaled and looked down at her feet as she remembered that late afternoon visit.

Treaz sat at her grandmother's bedside in the neighborhood nursing facility. They had picked the home out together over a decade earlier because it was small and intimate. Eight elderly residents, each with their own bedroom and bathroom. Four caregivers rotated shifts keeping the house clean, providing decent meals, and ensuring a safe environment.

"It's my birthday today," Treaz said, holding her grandmother's wrinkled and age-spotted hand. Grammie gave a toothless grin. She had not been putting in her dentures for the past month. "Grammie, where are your teeth?"

"No need for 'em," she said in a heavy Romanian accent. "Not 'til a brawny, young ninety-year old stud moves in the room next door."

Treaz laughed at her grandmother's sense of humor still alive and active at ninety-three.

Grammie adjusted the two pillows behind her back then slapped her hand to her forehead and frowned. "Oh, I didn't get you anything."

Treaz smiled at her. "No worries. You're my gift."

"How old are you now?"

"The ripe old age of thirty-two."

Her grandmother stayed silent as her grayish-blue eyes moved to dredge something up. "You and your boy doing something special?"

Treaz swallowed. "We broke up, remember?"

"You should get him back. He seemed like such a nice young man."

She caressed her grandmother's arm. "I can't do that, Grammie." A few moments of silence passed. "Hey, I had the strangest dream last night."

Grammie's eyes opened wider. "Oh?"

Sharing their dreams had become a beloved tradition between grandmother and granddaughter from their early years. They pieced together and described to each other seemingly senseless nightly experiences. Grammie theorized outlandish explanations of dreams perhaps developing from her own grandmother's old-world meanings, but regardless, Treaz found Grammie's interpretations fascinating.

"I took all these trips to weird places and was around people that I acted like I knew, but really didn't," said Treaz, unsure if Grammie followed much of the conversation anymore.

Once done describing the nonsensical, mixed-up dream, instead of Grammie's standard, unconventional interpretation, she simply sighed. "Don't forget about me. Come back when you're done."

Treaz rose and stroked her grandmother's thinning, white hair. "It was just a dream. I'll be back tomorrow. I just couldn't come yesterday because of an interview for—"

Grammie grabbed Treaz's arm and squeezed hard. "You are strong Treaz. Stronger than your mother. It takes a tough one to accept this gift."

Often her grandmother's thoughts were jumbled, requiring unsuccessful attempts at deciphering what she might mean. Treaz

14

understood dementia did awful things to one's mind, but this behavior appeared odd even for Grammie. "What gift?"

"You must search the boxes, search the boxes. All of them."

Treaz patted the old woman's hand assuming she must be feeling guilty for not getting Treaz a birthday present. "It's okay, Grammie. I don't need anything."

Agitated and breathless, her grandmother insisted. "Look in the boxes. You must look in the boxes."

Treaz stroked the old woman's cheek wanting to calm her. "Alright, I'll look and find something. It's gonna be fine."

"Accept the gift. Search the boxes, Treaz. Accept...search..." Grammie urgently continued until her voice became a whisper and she finally fell asleep, her breath slow and rhythmic. Treaz observed her grandmother for several minutes, then gave her a kiss on the forehead. "I love you, Grammie." She tucked a few pairs of the old woman's blue socks in her purse and left.

"I had planned on staying longer at the nursing home," Treaz told the counselor. "But after Grammie became so upset, I thought it best to go." She rubbed her eyes. "Can I get some coffee?"

Stacy nodded. "Sure." She made a phone call to put in the request. "What happened next?"

"I started drinking."

Treaz pulled a half-empty bottle of vodka from the back of the freezer and a container of orange juice from the refrigerator thinking a screwdriver would work perfect and be fitting for her present mood. The first two drinks went down easily along with a plate of reheated chicken tenders. With no more orange juice, Treaz found an expired box of cranberry-apple juice and mixed it in with the vodka. It still tasted decent, but everything tasted acceptable by then.

Grammie had been so adamant about Treaz finding a birthday gift in her boxed belongings. She had to stop avoiding the emotional assignment and honor her grandmother's request. Rather than more vodka, she selected an alternate liquid courage for traveling down memory lane, and after dusting off a bottle of cabernet, she carried it along with a dusty glass into the spare bedroom to face the task at hand.

She filled the glass and drank heartily while eye-balling the three medium sized U-Haul boxes set against the wall. Treaz never found the fortitude to place them in the attic despite always insisting on a very tidy, clean home. It broke her heart moving her grandmother out of the home she had lived in for almost a half century, but she needed full-time care that Treaz was not qualified to handle. Plus watching her grow more frail and confused made Treaz cry constantly which was not healthy for either of them.

It seemed sad all the personal treasures collected during a lifetime could be reduced to fit into only a few boxes. She unfolded the lids, exposing contents of immeasurable sentimental value but little monetary worth. Treaz pushed through the items stopping to examine a few more closely.

She poured her second glass of cabernet when she saw the first and last doilies Grammie had crocheted. They were wrapped around the black crucifix belonging to Treaz's grandfather whom Treaz had never met. A dainty white handkerchief embroidered with pink and lavender daisies and the initials of Treaz's great-grandmother was hidden underneath. She wiped away the tears that increased with each additional sip of wine.

She complied with Grammie's request to search through everything, but didn't find anything new. In the corner of the last box, snuggled in a soft cloth bag, Treaz found her grandmother's wedding ring—a single, round cut diamond mounted on a gold band. Grammie had removed it because of her edema. Should Treaz ever get married, she wanted to have that ring around her finger. Also tucked inside the bag was a plain gold band which must have belonged to her grandfather who died before her birth, and a silver charm bracelet that Treaz's mother, Maria, wore daily. It made a cheerful tinkling sound. Maria told Treaz that a good friend of hers gifted her with it many years before. She only took it off while bathing or during tasks where it might be damaged.

"Do you still know where your friend is?" Treaz asked her mother as she watched her clip on the bracelet one morning. Maria sighed, fondled the charms, and shook her head.

Maria removed the bracelet permanently the day she was committed to the hospital. Rules would not allow her to take anything of value inside, so she left it with Grammie for safe keeping. It remained around Grammie's wrist every day until Treaz's mother died. Upon arrival home after the funeral, her grandmother took it off and never wore the bracelet again.

Treaz touched each tinkling charm from around the world— a tiny silver Eiffel Tower, a half-inch pewter rendition of the Parthenon, carefully painted miniature yellow tulips from Holland, and several more. The beautiful and unique piece of jewelry obviously held meaning to all who wore it. Treaz thought it would make the perfect birthday present, and with clumsy fingers, she fastened it around her wrist.

"Where is the bracelet now?" asked Stacy.

Treaz encircled her bare wrist, unsettled by her now missing charm bracelet. She let her head fall forward saddened by the loss of something so special to both her mother and grandmother. "It was taken, just like my clothes, my home, and my life." The man with the pearl earring popped into her thoughts, again. Clearly he had something to do with this. "I think that Pearl Man guy stole it."

Jennifer entered with the coffee and handed it to Treaz avoiding any eye-contact. Treaz knew she had intimidated the young woman who had just been trying to do her job.

The coffee smelled weird, but it was hot and she seriously needed the caffeine boost, so she gagged down three gulps.

"Tell me about Pearl Man," said Stacy.

Drunk, and battling both emotional and physical exhaustion after sifting through her grandmother's boxes, Treaz had skipped her nighttime shower. She focused on changing into her favorite gray sweatpants and navy blue sweatshirt without falling down.

She stumbled to her bedroom window to close the blinds and saw someone staring in at her. Treaz gripped the dresser to steady her swaying, and squinted her eyes to be sure the man was real. He stood motionless on her grass about ten yards away from her window. Her mouth opened. "What the…?"

The street lamp, coupled with the powerful house security light, provided a clear view of him. He had an athletic frame, a bald head, and dark eyes. The man looked fiftyish and vaguely familiar, but at that moment of fuzzy thinking Treaz could not figure out why. Might he be visiting a neighbor or looking to buy the house? No. He looked far creepier than that. And he was standing on her lawn! Should she do something? Call 9-1-1?

Her stomach flopped as he held unblinking eye-contact with her for ten seconds before turning to walk away. Getting a glance of a pearl earring in his left ear lobe, she was more convinced she'd seen him before. Had he been here…watching her?

She ensured the window was locked and snapped the blinds closed. Propping herself up against the wall, she wondered if he was a threat or just a pervert. Peeking again, the man no longer was in sight. Her dizziness bordered nausea and there would be no ability to process any more emotions for the night. Treaz fell into bed and immediately into a sound sleep. The wrist with the bracelet hung over the side of the mattress.

Treaz explained to Stacy. "It seems like I've seen him before, but I've never met him. He must have been following me because, after that, all this weird stuff happened. What kind of person steals somebody else's life?" She drank more of the bad coffee. "It feels like a bad episode of the X-files or something." She gestured at herself. "I just don't want to get stuck in this. Honestly, I think it's some awful trick being played on me."

"By Pearl Man?"

"Maybe."

Stacy looked up from the monitor. "Have you ever suffered from mental illness or is there any history in your family?"

Treaz shifted on the bed, preparing to receive the dreaded diagnosis. "My mother did have some psychological issues."

"Tell me a little about your mother, Treaz."

"She was always very overprotective. Like way more than other parents were."

"Can you give me an example?"

Treaz flipped back Danielle's red hair. "She demanded I sleep in her bed every night. At first that was wonderful, but once I got into second grade, I was scared someone at school would find out. Plus, I wanted my own space. One night after she fell asleep, I snuck into my own bed. I remember how good it felt. In the morning my mother was sleeping next to me. Then she began sleeping by me in my bedroom. After my eighth birthday, I finally convinced her to let me spend the night with a friend from school. You'd think I was leaving for college. She kept crying and seemed so frightened for no reason. I didn't understand and still don't, but I cancelled, knowing I couldn't leave her alone."

Stacy nodded. "Did friends sleep over at your house?"

"The one friend I had was afraid to stay over because she said my mother was kinda weird."

"Did your mother receive a formal diagnosis?"

Treaz drew in a long breath and exhaled. "Yes. Paranoid schizophrenia." Needing to convince herself she did not exhibit any of her mother's symptoms, Treaz had chosen to write a report on the disorder during a university psychology course. At the time of the assignment, that tested true. Yet now a different story had emerged—her own story. Despite the missing disorganization and catatonic behavior, her delusions were very obvious. Her image reflected somebody different, which highly agitated her. Who wouldn't be freaked out? "But, I don't have that," Treaz said confidently to the counselor, although she suspected it may be moving that direction.

Stacy ignored Treaz's claim. "What about your father?"

She shrugged. "I never found anything out about him. In third grade, I made the mistake of telling someone at school that I didn't know who my father was...well, kids are kids. They started calling my mother a slut."

"What happened?"

"I was angry and confused. I didn't even understand what a slut actually was, but I figured it had to be something bad."

Treaz recalled that night vividly.

After dinner, she approached her mother in the kitchen. "Mom, can you tell me anything about my dad?"

Her mother continued washing the dishes. "I told you before, Treaz. There isn't anything to tell. Did you get your homework done?"

"You must know something."

Maria turned around. "I said there is nothing else to say about your father."

Treaz's hands balled into fists. "Were you a slut?"

Instead of an answer or even a raised voice, Maria slapped her daughter across the face. Treaz stood holding her reddening cheek, shocked. Her mother had never struck her before.

"Go to bed," her mother said with a shaky voice, tears in her eyes.

Treaz ran upstairs, flopped on her bed, and wept. Maybe her mother WAS a slut—whatever that even meant. During the middle of the night, she felt her mother's warm body curl up behind her and soon heard Maria's soft snoring.

Treaz looked to Stacy. "I never asked her about my father again. I did ask my grandmother, but she had never met him. Years later, I opened up my Grammie's old Bible and saw a handwritten version of our family tree. Most generations had only one offspring. I recognized my mother's name—Maria Popa, and next to that my father's initials—BF, supposedly standing for 'boyfriend', followed by my formal name—Nadia Popa."

Stacy made more notes. "So you were bullied as a child."

It was true. "Yeah. About how abnormal my mother was and how she doted over me."

"Is your mother still alive?"

"She was committed to a mental institution at forty-three and died three years later. I was only nine and living with my grandmother."

The questions persisted. "Are you holding down a job?"

"I got fired."

Another round of clicks.

Treaz rolled her eyes, her frustration growing rapidly. The more she talked, the deeper the hole became that she was digging herself into, and she was gaining no answers.

"Would you admit to having increased stress in your life lately?" asked Stacy.

Is she kidding? "Living in a stranger's body isn't stressful enough?"

The counselor overlooked the sarcasm. "Are you encountering any sensory changes?"

"No" she lied, not wanting to acknowledge her blurred vision earlier, the taste of their coffee reminded her of burnt tar, and the smell of the unwashed sheets at Danielle's apartment reeked of stinky feet.

"Have you ever been diagnosed with a chemical imbalance?"

"No."

"Then, what do you think is happening?"

Treaz raised her voice. "Isn't that what you're supposed to tell me?" Stacy ignored the reaction and waited until Treaz continued. "I'm not sure. Something supernatural like angels or magic? Or an experiment? How about a really scary nightmare or sick practical joke?" She slumped, dropping her gaze to a gouge on the wall.

Stacy closed the laptop lid, and pushed the cart to the side. "You may recall from your mother's struggles that schizophrenia can be a combination of thought, mood, and anxiety disorders," she explained. "When someone begins a phase, they can have trouble remembering recent events and can become irrational. You've described losing three days, feeling anxious, and experiencing suspicious thoughts about your Pearl Man. Often people develop unwarranted fears about family members."

"I said I don't know him," said Treaz, adamantly.

The counselor put her hand on Treaz's forearm. "Treaz, I'm concerned. I'd like you to stay and talk to our psychiatrist in the morning."

"You mean stay overnight?"

Stacy nodded. "We have a room—"

"I don't want to stay," said Treaz, flatly.

"It's alright," said the counselor. "It's just for one night."

"But, I don't know if—"

"I'll schedule an appointment with Dr. Branson for first thing in the morning. He'll want to conduct a battery of tests, and will be able to help."

Treaz considered the request.

"We can give you something to help you sleep tonight," added Stacy. "You're looking rather exhausted."

Even though she didn't like the idea of staying, at least she would be in a clean bed. Fearing becoming like her mother, maybe it would be best to catch this early—as if it were a chest cold. She reasoned in her head at least she'd be safe from Pearl Man if he decided to show back up.

Treaz sighed. "Okay. But, just ONE night."

Stacy gave a reassuring smile. "You've made the right choice."

"I don't have any way to pay...I don't think."

"We'll work something out. I'll have Jennifer come back in and stay with you while I make the arrangements."

"I'll be okay by myself," said Treaz. "You can leave the door open. I don't know where I'd go anyway."

Stacy thought about it, then agreed. "We'll get you in your room as soon as possible."

Treaz didn't like the sound of "your" room. She hoped that it wasn't a mistake. Thirty minutes later, Stacy escorted Treaz down the hall, up an elevator, along another hall, and to a secured door with a sign: Psychiatric Unit.

3

TREAZ

Stacy punched numbers on a keypad and the door to the unit unlatched. The counselor held it open for Treaz to enter. Treaz stood frozen. Locking people out was acceptable, but being locked in was not. The thought of going behind bolted doors in a hospital ward conjured up visions of visiting her mother. She couldn't help but remember how lonely and helpless she had felt after never being away from her mother for even a single night.

"Mom," Treaz said during her first visit with her mother after she had been committed to the mental institution. "When are you coming home?"

Maria hugged her nine-year-old daughter too tightly. Treaz fought to breathe. "The doctor says I need to get better first."

"When?"

Using a trembling hand, her mother wiped Treaz's wet cheeks. "I don't know, Sweet Pea."

"Can I stay here with you?"

"No honey, you can't. You'll stay with Grammie for a little while. You must keep close to her just like you've stayed close to me. Never open the windows, and keep all the doors locked."

Treaz looked up at her mother. "Why?"

Maria glanced around the room at the other people and whispered in Treaz's ear. "Because you can't trust anyone—no one."

The girl sniffed. "Not even Grammie?"

"She is the only person. Ever. No one else." Maria grabbed and squeezed Treaz's hands hard. "Do you understand?"

Treaz had seen her mother agitated before so even though she truly did not understand, she nodded anyway.

"No, say it. Tell me you understand," shouted Maria, more frantic. "Promise me."

A male attendant walked over. "Maria?"

Her mother gave the man a horrified glare and pulled Treaz behind her. "You stay away from her."

"Maria," the man said. "I'm not going to hurt—"

"Move back!"

He took hold of Maria's arm firmly. She began flailing and yelling for him not to touch her daughter.

Treaz's grandmother grasped her granddaughter's dress and tugged backwards. Together, they watched a second man take hold of Maria's other arm and force her out of the room as she continued to scream for Treaz.

Turning to Grammie, Treaz sobbed in her grandmother's embrace. She hated that place. She hated the nurses. She hated the doctors that put her mother in that awful hospital.

Stacy placed her hand on Treaz's back, giving her a little nudge to bring her back to the present. "It's going to be alright. Don't be frightened. You'll be safe here."

Don't trust anyone, Treaz reminded herself as she inhaled a long breath trying to clear her mind. Like mother, like daughter. Maybe she should just live as Danielle. Surely she could pull herself together enough to accept the world of existing in filth and loving cats. Couldn't she? No! She wanted to see Grammie again, so she gritted her teeth and entered the door hearing a substantial click behind her.

Stacy escorted her to a large desk and motioned to a nurse. "This is Lindy. She'll help you get settled. Dr. Branson will meet with you first thing in the morning." She gave Treaz's hand a comforting pat and left.

Lindy was a short, plump woman with spiky, black hair. Her voice was deep and without emotion. "Checking in for a while, Danielle?"

A shiver ran through Treaz's temporary body. "Only tonight."

Lindy lifted a single eyebrow, like she'd heard it all before. "Uh-huh." She took her to a room with two twin beds—both neatly made with perfected corners. The nurse pointed at the one next to the barred window. "That's yours. The recreation room is at the end of the hall on the left."

Treaz exhaled, planning to remain in her room the rest of the day, get a good night's sleep, see Dr. Branson in the morning, and get the hell out of there. "What time will I see the doctor tomorrow?"

She shrugged. "He likes to golf in the mornings. You bring anything with you?"

Treaz shook her head. She wished for her familiar gray sweatpants and navy sweatshirt, yet they wouldn't have fit Danielle's tall, skinny body.

Lindy exited for a minute, soon reappearing with a new toothbrush, small tube of toothpaste, and the standard blue gown. "You can wear this."

She didn't want to don *that* garb. That was something for a sick person, and she was trying so hard not to be that person. Treaz draped it over the back of a chair.

A crash came from another room, and Lindy ran out.

Unsure what to do, Treaz perched on the assigned bed, hugging her knees to her chest. She thought about how scared her mother must have been in a mental facility. Several hours passed before Lindy led someone new into the room. So much for the private room. The woman was around her mid-thirties. Her face was devoid of color, eyes blank and distant, and her feet shuffled. She embraced a well-worn teddy bear.

Lindy tossed the overnight bag she was carrying on the empty bed. "You know the routine, Melody. This is Danielle."

Treaz cringed. That name made the whole circumstance feel worse. "Hi." No response came as the woman sat on her bed, her back facing them.

"Melody doesn't talk much," said Lindy. "It'll take a week to break through."

"I'm only here for one night," Treaz said, again.

Lindy rolled her eyes. "Oh, yes. I forgot."

"And, I want to be called Treaz, not Danielle."

Lindy raised her palm at her before disappearing. "Dinner's in twenty minutes. Melody can show you where."

Melody sat so still that Treaz thought she'd fallen asleep. When the wall clock read 6:05 pm, people walked past their partially open door. She realized her stomach was empty. She stood and came around to look at her motionless roommate's face. "It's dinnertime. Do you want to go?" The woman did not look up. "Melody?"

After a moment, Melody walked out of the room, still gripping the bear. Treaz trailed behind into a medium-sized room where twelve other patients sat at various tables for four. Some sat by themselves, some across from or next to others.

Treaz surveyed the dining hall. A volunteer bribed a man to eat by way of a child's game. One woman sat alone carrying on a complete two-sided conversation. Another man could not stop laughing hysterically at a re-run of Bonanza playing on the small television hung high in the corner of the room.

How did she allow herself to get talked into staying at this place? She didn't belong there. She should have come back to talk to Dr. Branson another time.

Melody selected a table and Treaz joined her. A kitchen worker delivered trays of food to each of them.

Treaz eyed the dinner trying to decide where to start. Skipping the droopy green salad with glistening pools of Italian dressing, and the unappetizing wax beans floating atop a brown broth, Treaz went for the chicken. She broke her plastic fork trying to cut it. Glancing around the room, she noticed everyone picking up the poultry with their fingers—diluted white sauce dripping down their arms. Treaz sighed, understanding why there were no real knives allowed in the psych ward. She picked up the chicken and attempted a bite, but it tasted so dry, she dropped it disgustingly back on her plate. Dessert remained her only option so she dunked the chocolate chip cookie in the cup of milk.

Melody gnawed on her cookie, taking tiny bites like a rabbit, causing crumbs to tumble down her shirt and all over the table.

"I used to do that with my grandmother's cookies because it made the sweetness seem to last longer." Treaz nodded at her discarded meal, continuing, "About the only thing worth eating in this gawdawful mess."

This attempt at blunt humor hit a nerve with Melody, and she smiled through crumb covered teeth.

"If my Grammie tried chewing that chicken, her dentures would get stuck."

Melody snorted, followed by coughing from inhaled crumbs.

"Sorry," said Treaz as she rose to pat her back.

She waved Treaz off. "It's okay."

Treaz experienced a tinge of pride for getting Melody to speak sooner than seven days like Lindy had claimed. "Do you come here often?" That was the wrong thing to say for more than one reason. "I didn't mean that like a pickup line or…"

Melody smiled again, then her face grew serious. "Only when things get really bad."

They returned to their room without talking. Sitting on their beds in silence, Melody cuddled her stuffed animal while Treaz watched the second hand travel around the clock that was not near as entertaining as Danielle's cat with the shifting eyes.

At least Melody knew when to come in for professional help, something Treaz had never done. She always tried to deal with her periodic bouts of depression and loneliness on her own—which wasn't all that effective. Maybe that was why she was there, she reasoned with herself.

At 7:35 pm, Lindy brought in two small paper containers each holding a couple of white capsules. She gave one to Melody who immediately took them with some water. The nurse came to Treaz. "This will help you rest, Danielle," she said.

"Treaz."

Lindy cocked her head. Treaz swallowed the sedatives without hesitation. Sleep sounded wonderful, and maybe she would wake up in the morning with things back to normal, though she had her doubts.

After Lindy left, Melody changed into pajamas from her bag and crawled into bed. Treaz took that as a sign it was bedtime. She slipped into the hospital gown and climbed into her own bed. They both waited for the sleep medication to take effect.

"I haven't seen you here before," said Melody.

Flat on her back, Treaz stared at the ceiling tiles. "No, I don't even live in this city."

"Are you on vacation?"

Uncertain at first if she should try and explain anything, she reasoned what could it hurt? Melody obviously had psychiatric issues and Treaz didn't know her nor would ever see her again. "I'm living in somebody else's body." She turned to her side expecting a reaction from Melody, but received only a nod like she understood. "I saw this guy with one pearl earring standing outside my window before I went to bed. Then I woke up in a strange woman's apartment looking just like her. Danielle is not my real name."

"Melody isn't my real name either."

Treaz sat up. "It isn't?"

"No," said Melody, also sitting. Her eyes now wide and bright.

Treaz's mind spun. Could Melody be in the same situation as her? Had they been brought there by that man for medical experiments? "Do you know Pearl Man?"

Melody thought. "Maybe."

"Have you woken up in a different body, too?"

The woman nodded.

There *was* something to this. "Really? Are you in your own body now?"

"I don't think so, but maybe," Melody said.

Perhaps Melody had been in this state for so long she lost track of who she actually was.

Melody stroked her bear's paw. "Have you ever woken up as a little girl?"

"No. This is the first time it's happened to me. What about you?"

Clenching her bear tighter, Melody lay back down, and soon her shoulders began shaking.

Treaz heard faint sobs. She hadn't meant to upset the woman. "What's wrong?"

With tears streaming down her face, Melody jumped straight to her feet, her voice almost guttural. "Where'd you send Violet?" Before Treaz could answer, Melody hovered three inches from her face. "What did you do with Violet?"

Treaz pushed back in the bed. This woman was not stable at all. "I don't know Violet."

Melody panted, spittle flying from her mouth. "You're lying. Where is she?"

Treaz raised her hands, afraid of what this woman might do. "Melody. I have no idea who you're talking about."

"I'll find her, then I'll come find you, Treaz or Danielle, or whatever your name is." She shoved her index finger into Treaz's chest. "You're gonna pay for what you did." Melody scowled at her before returning to her own bed.

This woman's insane. Her heart pounded and she said nothing else, hoping that Melody would fall asleep before her, since there was no telling what the woman was capable of doing as Treaz slept.

It might appear that Treaz was mad, but not compared to the people around her. She had to get out of there. Otherwise, she might head in that same direction. But with bars on the windows and locked doors, how could she possibly escape? Treaz must convince Dr. Branson that she was not crazy. But, won't that prove that she was? If she says she's not, that means she is. If she says she is, then she is. Why, oh why, was she here? What a bad idea to come.

Then, the sleeping pills kicked in.

When Treaz gained consciousness, it was morning, and she had restraints on her feet and hands.

Oh God. The experiments are going to begin.

4

OMANI

Omani's crutch caught the dining room table leg, and she went down with a crash. "Oh," she shrieked as she fell. She tried to catch herself, and her finger tangled in her necklace and it ripped off—the charm rolling across the floor. Sprawled out on the cold tile, she used her muscled arms and the limited movement in her weak legs to pull her body to the first crutch and used it to hook the second.

"Miss LaZarres," cried Fritter rushing into the room. "You must be more careful."

"Just another bruise."

Fritter, at almost seventy years old, got down on her hands and knees and crawled under the table to retrieve the fallen electronic tablet. The short, portly woman bumped her head and gave the furniture a few choice words. Omani stifled a chuckle. She tolerated Fritter, who had earned her nickname as a teenager due to her ability to master the perfect apple fritter. But she wasn't totally trustworthy, so Omani had to be careful what she told her.

Standing up, Fritter handed Omani the device. "You are not so young anymore. One of these times you will break a bone."

"Would you take me to the hospital?"

The woman frowned. "You know I cannot do that, but I would call the doctor."

Omani sighed. Her Uncle had everyone trained so well. Omani slipped the device into her over-the-shoulder baby sling that she used to carry items since her hands were busy with her crutches.

The tenured head cook rushed back to the kitchen. Omani rubbed her reddened neck, scooped up the damaged chain and examined it. Another one would need to be ordered from Mr. Bisch, the main and only supplier, when he came the next afternoon. She dropped it in her pocket. After hunting for a minute, she found the charm resting against a coat rack. Struggling to reach it with her crutch, she dragged it closer to her, snatched it up and dropped it next to the chain.

Omani looked at her watch. 3:00 pm. Good. He should be on his afternoon cigarette break since smoking was against the rules in the building.

"It's really bad for the computers and for people," Omani had said during her presentation not long after starting her job. "It makes everything smell. If you want me to run this place in the most effective way, this needs to be the rule."

Despite her Uncle Filip's disagreement on many of her suggestions, he had allowed her to set up three designated areas constructed around the building's exterior. Each covered, and heated or cooled, depending on the season, with the touch of a small panel. Today, the heaters would take the chill from the frigid air.

The employee's daily habits were very predictable, and Omani took advantage of that predictability for her mischievous endeavors. She hurried down a long corridor. A variety of paintings hung along the walls with perfectly positioned accent lights highlighting apparently famous artists—ones whom Omani never heard of, thanks to her restriction of exploring any cultural richness.

Past the last painting, she held her hand up to a palm scanner, gaining access beyond a solid oak door. The latch disengaged and the door swung open easily; a feature Omani arranged to be installed for all the doors throughout the building making it easier for her to pass with her crutches.

Proceeding down the sterile white hallway, she passed offices with department names on electronic plaques. She stopped at the fourth door marked Communications and swiped her badge to enter.

As expected, the Comm, as he was known, was not in his office. The room contained two desks with computers, some file cabinets, and a table with a coffee maker. She nodded approvingly at the insulated metal mug with a plastic lid sitting on the desk—a large letter "V" was printed on the side in red. It was one of Omani's recent ideas in an attempt to cut down on non-recyclable Styrofoam cups and wasted cold coffee. Mr. Bisch had delivered three boxes of the mugs last week.

She checked the time again. 3:06 pm. Leaning her crutches against the desk, she sat down in front of the computer facing the door. She hadn't snooped around for years, but recently she'd become more restless. Everyone in her Uncle's company seemed to be more energetic; maybe that was rubbing off on her as well. A touch to the tracking ball brought up a menu. Omani saw this many times on the Comm's monitor before, yet she had never tried going further to find out what it meant. Her heart pounded.

There were three options—Comm, Internal, External. The Comm choice would have to do with Communications work. Internal likely meant within her Uncle's business, and she certainly didn't need anyone inside knowing she was being nosy. External might mean she could get to the outside. Learning what was going on in the world would be fantastic since she didn't receive any news except for what she could weasel out of Mr. Bisch who didn't say much aside from an occasional comment about an election or natural disaster.

Omani bit her lip, wiped sweaty hands across her lap, and selected External. She was right. Her eyes scanned the screen, packed with information—so much information. She chose a photograph of a nice looking young man. The headline announced his recently declared candidacy for Parliament representing the Swiss Green Liberal Party. The story was interesting, but not what she wanted to spend her precious time reading. Omani hit the back arrow. Her knowledge of technology was pretty rusty with her own machine being limited to basic databases, spreadsheets, and syncing with her electronic pad for work tasks.

One more glance at the clock. 3:12 pm. She suspected the Comm would return soon, but her curiosity moved her to the first menu option—Comm. A window popped up revealing an empty space with a border surrounding it, and a button that read "Encrypt".

A swiping sound and clunk of the unlatching door startled Omani. She clicked back and jumped up. As the man entered, she ran her hand across the top of the monitor noting imaginary dust.

"What are you doing?" he demanded, surprised at her presence.

Without making eye-contact, she consulted her finger, then pulled her device out to make a note. "Quality check."

"On what?"

"Housekeeping. Been having some problems." She put the crutches under her arms. "Let me know if you have any issues." She felt his gaze upon her as she exited, but he said nothing. That was close. A smirk came across her face. Omani had forgotten the thrill of almost getting caught doing something her Uncle would forbid. She wanted to do more. There was a new guy, Rafael, starting soon in Information Technology. Yesterday, she had prepared his ID badge and delivered it to the head of IT. It would be fun engaging her talents of persuasion to see what she might find out from him before her Uncle's unreasonable rules of seclusion began.

5

OMANI

At the end of her work day and after her solitary dinner, Omani went back to her modestly-sized living unit. Outside the door she picked up two bags of neatly folded clothes. She hooked them around her arm and carried them inside. Twice a year Omani was given cash to purchase clothing. Since she was unable to enjoy a shopping trip herself, she would ask one of her housekeeping employees if they would pick up the needed items. It was embarrassing to obtain her clothes that way, not being able to choose them for herself. However there were no other alternatives aside from wearing the same attire for decades. Sometimes the patterned shirts and skirts they picked up were not really to her liking, but she was grateful for anything new.

After hanging up her new clothes, she slipped off her shoes and changed into a blue cotton, floor-length nightgown with a pattern of puppies sleeping, eating, and playing—the result of a previous well-meaning shopper. Omani pondered herself in the mirror. The choice of bedtime clothing humorously summed up her life, except replace the playing puppies with working dogs.

Touching the bruise now forming on her hip from the earlier fall, Omani yanked open the dresser drawer and removed two small grey pills from a bottle. Her lower legs ached. She didn't like taking the pain medication on a regular basis, but after the tumble and being on her feet all day, it was definitely warranted. Then she headed for her go-to comfort food. She sucked on spoonfuls of chocolate chunk gelato, savoring the flavor and chewing the frozen candy. Omani had developed the skill of savoring after heeding her mother's relentless instruction on the proper way to consume the delicacy.

"You can make it last longer if you eat it slower," said her mother. "That also means that you will consume less because as you age, those extra pounds will be harder to shed."

"Oh Momma. I'm only eight. It'll be forever 'til I'm old like you."

Hanna stifled a laugh. "You just wait, young lady."

"Do you think I've stopped growing yet?"

"I certainly hope not." Omani sighed dramatically. "You're too impatient," said her mother.

Omani was tired of crutches. It would be so wonderful to be able to run and jump like all the other girls. "I don't want to wait until I'm eighteen," she whined. "You're a doctor. Can't you make it work sooner?"

"If I could, I would, Ani. It's hard, but as we've discussed before, it's best you stop growing before having the surgery." Hanna put her arm around her daughter. "I'm so sorry about that car accident."

Omani shrugged. "I don't remember it."

"I know, but I'm just sorry that it happened at all." Omani swallowed another huge bite of gelato. Her mother waved her hands. "Savor, Omani. Savor."

Thinking about her mother reminded Omani of the broken necklace, and she retrieved it from the pocket of her skirt.

Rubbing the pewter ladybug between her fingers, she thought back to the day she acquired the treasure.

After Omani's school friends had left from her tenth birthday party, and she was readying herself to devour the first chapter of a new fantasy novel, *The Reckoning of Planet 62*, she had received from Julia, Hanna sat down on the couch next to her.

"Hi, Momma."

"Hi, Daughter." Then she handed Omani a small box with a yellow bow. "Happy birthday, Ani. Welcome to double digits."

Omani grinned and inspected the gift. Soon the ribbon was tugged off, paper torn, and lid opened. She removed a pewter-based, red and black ladybug charm on a chain. " Oooh, so pretty. I love it. Here." She put the necklace against her chest holding the ends out for her mother to link the clasp.

"Ladybugs are very special. They symbolize good fortune and prosperity," said Hanna. "Their colors represent the importance of living a life full of joy."

"I'll never take it off."

Hanna laughed. "Well, you might want to—"

"No. Every day forever." Omani hugged her mother. "Thank you, Momma. It's the best present ever."

Omani had kept her promise. She might not be able to wear her beloved necklace for a few days, but being the only possession she had left from her mother, it would remain close. She placed the charm and chain on her bed stand.

She brushed her teeth, washed her face, then went to stare out of the window—her typical nightly routine. Omani gazed at the dark outline of the Swiss Alps. The bright moon created tree shadows across the snowy hillside. Despite her isolation in such a rural location, her mother had taught her to appreciate beauty in nature—both in the colorful flowers of summer and the freezing snow caps in winter. Often she envisioned herself traipsing across those treacherous mountains on a quest to get far away from her existing life. But for a woman unable to walk without the aid of crutches, that type of story remained possible only in her novel reading.

After crawling into bed, Omani picked up a half-read book and spent the balance of the evening absorbed in the world of beautiful Lady LeiLani—warrior, explorer, and heroine who traveled worlds in both space and time. Lady LeiLani had just returned to a time three hundred years earlier to fight the multi-generational battle of her ancestors. Regardless of being long past her teenage years, Omani had never outgrown her love of young adult fantasy.

6

TREAZ

Treaz pulled and tugged, trying to free herself from the restraints on the bed. Melody was absent, her bed made, suitcase and stuffed bear gone. A hollowness developed in Treaz's gut as she called for help—faintly at first, then louder. "Help me." She couldn't breathe, her heart pounded, and an intense feeling of doom overcame her. Her hands and feet tingled, and body trembled. "Somebody help me!" she screamed.

A new nurse strolled in the room with a cheery disposition. "Morning. Time to rise and shine." She cranked open the blinds creating a swatch of blinding sunshine.

Out of breath, Treaz squeezed her eyes closed, confused at how she might abide by the nurse's request while being bound to the bed.

The nurse came to stand next to her. "It's alright. Sometimes people have panic attacks when they are restrained."

No kidding. "Can you get them off?"

"What's your name, hon?"

"Treaz."

The woman folded her arms across her chest and tilted her head.

"Danielle Edwards."

The nurse nodded in approval, and removed the straps.

"Where's Lindy?"

"Shift change. Can't work twenty-four seven, you know."

Treaz rubbed her wrists and sat up. "Why'd she tie me up?"

"Rough night?"

"I'm not sure."

The nurse went to a cupboard and shuffled around. "Apparently, you threatened your roommate."

Treaz frowned. "That's not true."

"Melody had scratch marks on her back."

"I didn't do that."

The nurse held out a towel and fresh gown. "Shower time."

"I want my own clothes."

"Sorry, no can do," she said walking to the door and pointing down the hall. "Shower's second door on the left."

She selected a stall as far from the female monitoring the area as possible. The door barely gave her enough privacy—her body was so tall. She stood under a dribble of lukewarm water wondering what happened after she went to sleep. Surely she wouldn't have hurt Melody. This place was making her insane. The sooner she could see the psychiatrist and leave, the better. She finished quickly, toweled off, and pulled the heavily starched clean blue gown on in the tiny enclosure bumping her elbows multiple times.

After opting out of breakfast, two hours later, she was ushered into another neat office where a man was working at his desk.

He stood and shook her hand. "Good morning, Danielle. Make yourself comfortable."

Treaz sat, choosing not to correct him on her name.

"My name is Dr. Branson. I read what Stacy wrote; what you discussed with her yesterday. How are you doing, today?"

"Much better, thank you," she lied. "Look, I think there's a misunderstanding as to why I'm here."

He cocked his head. "What's that, Danielle?"

"I didn't want to stay, but Stacy insisted it would be safer."

Dr. Branson consulted his monitor. "From Pearl Man?"

Treaz dug a thumb nail into the side of her index finger. Her mom had warned her not to trust anyone! She wished she hadn't said so much to that counselor. "No, he's fine, really. I'm doing better now, and I need to get back to work." She smiled dryly. "Can't be late."

"The job you were fired from?"

Treaz stood, and paced across his office.

"In my professional opinion, I feel it imperative that you remain another night or two for observation and further assessment. Then we can discuss the best course of action."

She stopped in front of a shelf filled with medical books, including all the published volumes of the *Diagnostic and Statistical Manual of Mental Disorders (DSM)*. Treaz recognized the DSM-IV textbook she used during her college psychology class to research her mother's illness. "Look, I don't belong here. I was just mixed up, yesterday. I partied a little too much on my birthday. Bad me."

Dr. Branson stared as she ranted.

"I am not a crazy person," she said, a little too harshly.

"We don't like to use those terms, Danielle. How would you explain your actions last night?"

"That woman you put me with threatened me."

The doctor interlocked his fingers. "Melody is not aggressive."

"Well, she was to me. I was scared to fall asleep. And then I'm the one who got tied down."

"We only restrain patients—"

"I'm not a patient!"

Dr. Branson exhaled. "Please, sit down, Danielle."

Treaz reluctantly complied.

"I understand your mother was diagnosed with—"

"My mother had a disease. But I told you, I'm better now."

"I find it troubling that your behavior appears to be erratic and combative. You are showing classic symptoms of paranoid schizophrenia, like your mother. This disorder which is often hereditary can be managed with suitable medications and psychosocial therapies. There is no shame in recognizing our mental health issues and in reaching out for support. We are here to help you, Danielle."

"My name is not Danielle!"

Dr. Branson arched his eyebrows and focused his attention on the monitor on his desk. His phone vibrated and he looked at it. "Excuse me a moment...Dr. Branson...I'll be right there." He got up. "Will you be alright for a few minutes, Danielle?"

"Of course."

He exited the room, leaving the door wide open so that his assistant could keep a watchful eye on her.

Treaz went to the window. There were no bars but also no way to open it. She entertained the thought of smashing the glass and jumping from the fourth floor. Two broken ankles seemed worth it to escape from Dr. Branson and his prison. She shivered and sat down rubbing her wrist where the bracelet had hung. It was lost, just like Treaz.

Footsteps brought Treaz back to the present. The doctor reappeared with a smile. "Good news."

She turned. What could possibly be good news?

"You're able to go home after all."

Externally, she smiled. "Great." Internally, she was puzzled. Go home? Home to where? Danielle's crummy apartment? It didn't matter. She was thrilled to flee that place.

"You were lucky your uncle found you. I had a nice chat with him and he assured me he was well aware of your issues. He's waiting downstairs."

Treaz was dumbfounded. She didn't have an uncle. Wait. It must be Danielle Edward's uncle. At that point, she didn't care who showed up to get her, because there was no way she wanted to lose the chance to bolt from that facility.

"Now Danielle, I highly recommend you return for regular counseling sessions either with us or another provider." Dr. Branson handed her a business card. "I'll give your nurse a prescription for a low dosage of Olanzapine. That should begin to ease your delusions and hallucinations, but you must establish yourself with a psychiatrist. Call if you'd like to schedule with our facility."

Treaz nodded. *Fat chance.*

"It is essential that you attain a full evaluation for long-term management. Do not stop taking the medication, otherwise it will likely lead to a relapse of your symptoms. If you stick to proper treatment, you can live a happy and successful life."

"Fine."

"I explained all this information to your uncle. He said he would make sure you followed through on our suggestions."

Returning to her room, she changed back into Danielle's smelly clothes that had mysteriously reappeared on her bed.

Lindy stopped in. "Leaving us so soon?"

"I told you I was only staying for one night," said Treaz, an edge in her tone.

"Oh, we'll see you, again," said the nurse. She gave her the prescription and a printout. "Let me grab your paperwork and you'll be on your way." She scurried out of the room.

Treaz perused the paper, her eyes widening at the first paragraph. It summarized the possible side-effects of the medicine.

Mild effects are dry mouth, blurred vision, constipation, drowsiness and dizziness. More severe effects are trouble with muscle control, muscle spasms or cramps in the head and neck, and shuffling of the feet. With prolonged use the patient can suffer from facial tics, thrusting and rolling of the tongue, lip licking, panting and grimacing.

Wow. Treaz didn't believe she needed to be on such strong medication, but Dr. Branson had concerned her enough that perhaps she should consider it.

The nurse returned. As Treaz signed the discharge form, Lindy pulled the sheets off the beds and piled them in the corner. "A volunteer's on their way to escort you out."

Treaz protested, insisting she could manage by herself.

"Rules are rules."

Ten minutes later a volunteer came to escort Treaz from the psychiatric unit, down the elevator, and to the Caring Hearts Hospital lobby.

Once there, her hands squeezed into fists. She recalled Stacy telling her the day before, "Often people have unwarranted fears about family members." Treaz instantly recognized the man claiming to be her uncle.

7

TREAZ

In a split second, Treaz had to make the decision if she would stay in that horrible place or go with the man she described as stalking her. Pearl Man stood across the lobby. *Who was that guy?* Surely if she went with him, she could find an opportunity to run away. If he didn't kill her first, he at least might have an explanation. She walked straight up to him, for the first time grateful to be in Danielle's tall body. Being almost at eye-level, Treaz looked him in the eye.

"I'm fairly sure you have questions," he said.

Sarcasm filled her voice. "That's an understatement. I saw you outside my house. I've seen you before, somewhere. How do I know you?"

"You don't." He turned, and Treaz followed him out the door. As they walked, Pearl Man snatched the prescription and business card from her hand and dropped them in a trash receptacle. "You won't be needing those."

They stopped next to a white Ford Explorer in the parking lot. He swung open the passenger door. She hesitated. "Uh, I'm not getting in there until you explain what's going on and who you are."

He nodded. "Smart young woman. I won't hurt you, Treaz."

He said her name. He knows her. That alone proved she wasn't crazy. She wasn't falling into the throws of paranoid schizophrenia. It wasn't a Romanian curse. She wasn't dreaming. A wave of cautious relief flushed over her as she realized she wasn't losing her mind. "Who are you, then?"

"The doctor said you called me Pearl Man." He twisted his earring. "That works."

"Alright, Pearl Man. I'd really like to know what is going on," she pointed to her body, "and who this is?"

"Ah yes. It's confusing," he said.

She smirked. "No kidding."

"You have a very important job to do."

"I had a job in my old life."

He lifted his eyebrows.

"Well, up until I got fired for no reason a few weeks ago. Did you have something to do with that, too?"

Pearl Man retrieved his keys. "Now you have two jobs."

Treaz cocked her head. "Great. And why do I need more than one?"

"The Host's employment, in your case that's Danielle, is only a means to an end. The job you do for us is primary."

She threw her hands up. "Do you guys not pay me enough or something?"

He smiled. "There is no compensation."

Confused, Treaz shook her head. "What? Why would I want to work for your company for nothing?"

Pearl Man winked at her. "You get free room and board."

Was this an attempt at humor? Here she was occupying Danielle's body, living in her apartment, hijacking her life. "That's not funny."

He bit his lip. "Sorry." Again, he motioned for her to enter the vehicle. "Please. I'll share what I can."

Treaz took in the interior. Not a spec of dirt, empty fast-food bag, or discarded water bottle anywhere. "Where do you want to take me?"

"Home."

"My home? In San Antonio?"

Pearl Man grimaced. "Unfortunately not."

She already knew the answer was Danielle's place. Could she actually cooperate with the man who put her in this terrible situation to begin with? But, surprisingly, he seemed to be an okay guy—for a likely psychopath. She blew out a breath, got in the car, and placed her finger over the door's unlock button after Pearl Man closed her door. They pulled away.

"If I'm in this body, is Danielle in mine?"

He shook his head. "No."

Was Danielle safe? Was she dead? "Where'd she go and where's my body?" Pearl Man ignored her questions. Treaz was afraid to push further.

"Think of this as an opportunity," he said.

"I don't even understand what THIS is. What am I supposed to do?"

"You'll be focused on finding a particular individual, who we call an Asset."

She turned to face him. "How will I know who it is?"

"I can't tell you that. You're to help him or her accomplish something."

"You mean like wash their car?"

He chuckled. "You'll need to determine that."

Treaz rolled her eyes. "That sounds pretty cryptic and like a whole lot more work. Why can't you just tell me?"

Pearl Man shrugged. "That's the way things operate."

"What happens if I refuse?"

He pinched the clasp on his earring tighter. "Just try it first."

51

"Can I go home after that?"

"You'll return after finishing your final assignment."

Treaz exhaled a long breath. At least she'd be going home once her work was finished. An hour from then wouldn't be soon enough. She decided it best to go along to ensure there wasn't a repeat trip back to the *caring hearts* of Dr. Branson and nurse Lindy. "Do I have a title?"

"You are a Transitioner. You'll be using your ability to influence people."

"Oh no. Is this a sales position?"

He gave a twisted smile. "You might think of it that way. Yet, you're not selling a product."

"Can I take a few more days off?" Treaz asked, not sure of her readiness to start new employment right away. "I need some time to think this over."

"You've been given ample time to adjust. Now you must get to work."

They pulled into the apartment complex, and he shifted the car in park. She sat silent for a moment gazing at the building where everything had started the morning before. Her stomach twisted—a combination of hunger and trepidation about returning. The only thing she was certain about, was she wasn't certain about anything—except who she was on the inside. "I honestly don't feel nuts anymore after being in that hospital."

"Don't second guess yourself."

Familiarity brought a smile to her face. "My grandmother used to say to always trust my gut."

"Very wise." Reaching in the back, he rummaged in a briefcase for something.

"Is this some kind of gift from God?"

Pearl Man glanced at his watch. "Enough for today." He handed her a small packet. "These will help you sleep. It can be hard to turn off the brain the first few days, believe me."

She looked at him. Maybe he wouldn't be too bad of a boss. "Thanks for getting me out of that place."

He nodded.

"Why didn't you come tell me all this sooner?"

"I have others to attend to," he explained. "It would do you good to be more patient, Treaz."

She pushed the door open and stepped out. "Pearl Man, how do I reach you?"

"I'll find you."

She slammed the door, then knocked on the glass. He lowered it. "Hey, which apartment is my free one?"

"Third floor, second on the left."

"What do I do now?"

"Don't be late for work," said Pearl Man as he rolled up the window and drove away.

She rubbed her forehead while watching his car disappear around the corner. How will she figure out what to do? What kind of new job didn't offer any training? And, the bigger question, how was being in someone else's body even possible? Exasperated at so many unanswered questions, she wasn't sure how she would handle things, but she needed to go along with Pearl Man's instructions if she wanted to return to her former life. That much she understood.

Treaz trudged upstairs to Danielle's unit. The door had been left unlocked and, when she entered, her hands went to her hips at the state of the apartment. She could never live in such a mess. A hot shower might clear her head.

She scrubbed herself hard in an almost scalding flow of water, hoping in some way to *scrub* off the offending new person

53

and her freckles. Isn't that what people did after a crime scene or if something awful happened to them, they cleansed everything away? She felt a little pinch on the inside of her upper right arm and ran her finger over a tender, red scratch. "Ow."

The cleansing gel scent reminded Treaz of sitting in Grammie's favorite chair, which she did quite frequently. The mustard yellow rocker still smelled like her—not repugnant or musty, but of her beloved Joy, a pricy perfume popular in the 1930s. She recalled Grammie telling her the story about how on her eighteenth birthday, her mother gave her her first bottle of Joy coupled with strict motherly direction. "Now that you're a woman, Elena, you need to start looking for a man."

Treaz loved the fragrance and, although she didn't wear perfume, she did keep her small front yard trimmed and brimming with jasmine and roses, reminiscent of the sweet flowery scent. Grammie never changed perfumes and continued to douse it on daily until she moved into the nursing home where she wasn't allowed to use Joy any longer and forced to accept a more antiseptic aroma.

Her tears blended with the now cooling water, so she shut off the faucet, and dried with an offensive smelling, tattered towel. She pulled down the sheet she had hung yesterday morning, tentatively wiping away the condensation from the bathroom mirror. The strange young woman with the green eyes still stared back at her.

Treaz sighed. "I'm not insane. I'm not my mother."

She went to search the battered old dresser for undergarments, which she found in the lowest drawer. *Who doesn't keep their underwear in the top drawer?* Thankfully there were laundered ones and she slipped them on, all the while pushing down her disgust of wearing a strange woman's panties, clean or not. She opted out of the ragged bra—this body could manage without one. Treaz picked out a blue pair of socks, thinking back to her last visit with Grammie. Every other day Grammie asked for socks.

The old lady would wiggle her toes under the bed-covers. "Can you buy me some socks, dear? My feet are always cold here."

Swallowing a chuckle, Treaz would do what she did every time she left the home—sneak out a few pairs of her grandmother's standard blue ones and bring them back the next day as a welcomed surprise.

Treaz ached for her grandmother and dreaded receiving the anticipated news that would change things forever. Life would be difficult without Grammie.

The closet held a multitude of frilly dresses and fashionably ripped jeans. Despite inheriting her stoutness from her mother, it wouldn't matter because Danielle's clothes would fit. Nothing in Treaz's style, but then again, she wasn't herself. She pulled on pants and a long-sleeved tee-shirt carrying the least worn smell.

Treaz never cared for cats, yet found herself smiling at the cute kittens on the wall posters. What was this sudden new affection for these furry creatures? She wondered who Danielle might be. By the appearance of her barren apartment, she obviously didn't make a ton of money. She lived alone though, so she must be scraping by.

In the living room Treaz found nothing out of the ordinary for someone who spent too much time glowering over felines and reading gossip magazines when they should have been doing housework. She spent the rest of the afternoon and evening flipping television channels desperately seeking distraction. Nothing held her attention. Again, she thought about calling her grandmother, but even if Grammie was still alive, what could Treaz possibly say? *I awoke in another woman's body and a man with a pearl earring is responsible.* That screamed insanity. She would wait until things got figured out with Pearl Man.

Eventually she changed into Danielle's pajamas, got into bed, and tossed for at least an hour before remembering the sleeping pills Pearl Man had given her. She swallowed two and finally fell asleep—her night void of any dreams.

8

OMANI

Mr. Bisch showed up at his regular time the following day. The supplier was never late, ever. In his mid-sixties, he wore a perpetual frown causing deep wrinkles between his eyes and making his long nose appear even longer. There were ways to look more youthful, but he either couldn't afford them or opted to not hide the gray in his hair or lines on his face.

"Good afternoon, Mr. Bisch."

"Hmph," he grunted. "Maybe for you."

That was Mr. Bisch; his grumpiness a constant she grew to expect. Long ago she decided to not allow him to intimidate or bring her down; instead choosing to be amused by his attitude. In a strange way, she liked his demeanor because he remained one of very few people that she could talk to—even if only about work. He showed up frequently to deliver supplies for maintenance, housekeeping, and office needs, and also take the next order.

She held up her broken jewelry.

He donned thick glasses. "What the hell is that?"

"A ladybug. Can you get me another chain?"

He nodded. "I gotta place. Guaranteed it won't bust again."

Two of his employees emerged from the truck and began unloading previously purchased items while he and Omani spent their typical ninety minutes together walking the entire campus discussing needed upgraded shower heads or closet doors, new carpeting, or a paint refresh. These were chores that maintenance workers would handle, but they'd need supplies. The original single story, thirty thousand square foot building had slowly expanded to two-stories bringing it to over sixty thousand, mostly based upon Omani's planning and oversight for Filip's business offices, meeting rooms, storage facilities, and sleeping quarters.

Her Uncle employed seventy-three people, at Omani's last count. Most of them worked a schedule of three weeks in a row, then they left for the fourth week—except for Omani, of course. She never left. Although she couldn't view financial information for the company, she imagined that all Filip's direct reports were well compensated. Her own assigned budget for wages was minimal, forcing her to spread it as best she could across her staff. Many of them worked to support families living in France, Germany, and Austria. Omani disliked that Filip took advantage of these individuals, but most were thankful to have scored jobs at all.

Omani insisted on her own modest living unit along the same hall as the employees she supervised, far away from her Uncle. Filip's staff enjoyed living arrangements much more luxurious— each outfitted with sixty-inch QLED televisions, floor to ceiling windows, marble counters in full kitchens, and Jacuzzi bathtubs in bathrooms big enough to fit Omani's entire room.

A well-dressed man stepped from his suite while peering at a shiny, new electronic device. He looked up. "Oh, hey."

"Hello, Rafael," said Omani. "This is Mr. Bisch, our supplier."

The men shook hands.

"You settled in?" she asked.

"The daily housekeeping's cool." He scrunched his face. "But, I'm still getting lost."

She chuckled and nodded. "It does take a while to find your way around."

"No kidding," said Rafael. "Did you receive those computer replacement parts?"

"Just ordered them today. Should be in the next order we get," she confirmed.

"Okay. Let me know when they arrive and I'll stop by to get everything fixed up for you."

It was vital Omani get as much out of Rafael as she could before he began to abide by Uncle Filip's number one unwritten rule—don't become friends with his niece.

Omani led Mr. Bisch out to one of the less popular exterior smoking spots. She eyed the space, drawn in by its solitude. Over the years, she had shed many lonely tears there. "I want to change the walls from this ugly brown to a bright ocean blue. I've got money in my budget for all three areas."

He cocked his head and pulled up paint samples on his tablet. "Like this?"

She grimaced at the dark navy. "No, brighter like the color in the Caribbean."

"Never been," Mr. Bisch said.

Omani exhaled. "Me neither." The small lake on the property provided a calm, serene, reflecting place during the summer months, but come winter, the lake froze making it too dangerous to maneuver with her crutches. Omani pointed at a color called Aqua Quartz. "That one."

Their last destination was Filip's huge corner office. His windows offered bird's eye views of the sprawling grounds. They passed the heavy mahogany desk with leather chairs, a lengthy wet bar, several well-polished cupboards. Omani knew they were

59

locked because she tried them whenever she was in there alone in hopes one might be inadvertently left open. No such luck.

One of the glass doors to the massive stone fireplace had been shattered allowing a cold draft to flow in past the shards still dangling from the frame. Mr. Bisch arched a brow and logged the measurement for the replacement piece. He didn't ask what happened. Most of the time she had no explanation herself.

Back at Mr. Bisch's truck, Omani fished some crumpled papers from her over-the-shoulder sling and handed them to Mr. Bisch. He frowned. "Sorry, my printer jammed." She understood his frustration taking the food supply requests the old fashioned way. He had voiced his opinion about that more than once. Omani just shook her head. Filip forbade her any contact with the outside world including making routine orders online, telling her it was for her own protection.

Omani bid her usual sentiment. "Thanks Mr. Bisch. Have a nice week."

His response was always the same. "Hmph." He might as well have said, "I love you, too." He was a friend of sorts.

Her stomach growled. She had forgotten to eat lunch again. She headed towards the kitchen thinking about always being hungry as a teenager.

At fourteen, Omani went to their home office to pester her mom and Julia, her mother's best friend. She dropped her crutches and flopped into a bean bag chair. "Mom, let's go eat. I'm starving."

"You're always starving," laughed Hanna.

"Every teenager is starving," chided Julia.

Omani picked up a paper from Hanna's desk and scanned it haphazardly, not really paying much attention. "Come on, let's go to Shelby's for dinner."

Hanna swiped the document from Omani's hand. "Julia and I are working."

Omani tossed her head back and groaned. "You guys are always working. Don't you wanna take your daughter for her favorite burger and cheesy fries?"

Hanna looked at Omani, smiled, and went back to her typing.

"Mom, pleeeeeease?"

"I should probably get home anyway, Hanna," said Julia. "My husband will be happy for a home-cooked meal tonight. You two go and enjoy."

Hanna exhaled and turned off her monitor. "Alright. Go put your shoes on."

Omani shot both arms up. "Yes!"

Forty-five minutes later, Omani and Hanna sat at the counter at Shelby's, an American restaurant. They were regulars, and the serving staff always made a point to stop by to chat whenever they came in. Omani loved watching the chefs flip the burgers and pour freshly melted cheddar cheese over the fries, smothering them. Everyone seemed to love Hanna no matter where they went, and they appeared to like Omani too, because she was Hanna's daughter.

Hanna watched her daughter shovel four sloppy fries into her mouth at once. "You realize how many calories—"

"Seriously? Don't ruin it. We should come here at least three times a week." Her mother laughed. "Okay. How about every time you and Julia work late?"

"What kind of crazy idea is that, Ani?"

Omani wiped cheese from her chin and sat forward. "You're always working on your science or math project or whatever every single night. When are you gonna be done?"

Hanna cocked her head. "It won't be over until it's over."

"That's such a cop-out, Mom."

"Research takes time."

Omani chewed on her last french fry. The one drenched the heaviest in cheese. "Who are you hoping to find? Aliens?"

Hanna chuckled. "You never know. Likely people in a different land via new technology."

"Why don't you just use the phone?" asked Omani.

"We're searching for another way." Her mother leaned in and winked. "And who knows, maybe even another planet."

"Right," Omani rolled her eyes. "Hey, can we stop for gelato?"

Omani entered the Research offices after hours, responding to a work order placed earlier that day. The bulk of Filip's employees worked in Research. Omani supposed they concentrated on tracking terrorist activities—her Uncle's claimed primary concern. Indeed, the wood laminate on the front of one of the desks gaped open. The employee tried to use tape and glue, but nothing held. She noted on her tablet to replace the workstation altogether.

Under the desk she noticed a partially shredded paper protruding from the machine. Pushing the button only caused a grinding noise but no movement. It was full. Omani emptied the long paper shreds, and wrote a reminder to tell the housekeeping staff to check all shredders daily as sometimes they got lazy, refusing to empty the machines and leaving scraps all over the floor. She put the half-shredded piece back in the machine to finish the job but stopped. Perhaps she'd find something interesting. *If it was being destroyed, it must be confidential.* She folded and slipped it in her pocket to review later and completed her furniture inspections.

Back in her room, she read the paper from the shredder. The article was about an American student, who, years before, got caught breaking into a college laboratory and hacked into the school computers. Excessive blood-alcohol levels didn't help his defense, and he'd been expelled despite being a straight 'A' engineering major.

Such a waste of potential for young…

the story read before leading into unreadable fragments.

Omani wondered why Research would be interested in him. Might he be a suspected terrorist? Of course, the article was meant to be shredded, so maybe he didn't pan out to be a credible threat.

She reached behind her desk and removed a secret lock box. Entering a combination, the top clicked open revealing a green folder. She had established the file years ago after a supplier had found and handed her a dusty, crinkled paper from behind an old desk being replaced. Omani had glanced at the list of names with half of them marked through. Were they potential future clients of Filip or bad people? She decided to start her own Green Mystery Folder like her mother had kept in a locked drawer when Omani was a young girl.

"Momma?" Omani had asked one time. "What do you keep in that green file?"

"Oh, just bits and pieces."

"Can I see?"

Hanna smiled and shook her head. "Not now, baby girl. When you're older."

"But why not?"

Her mother stroked Omani's hair. "You're a curious one, aren't you?"

"Is that bad?"

"Definitely not. Never stop asking questions."

From that day on, Omani dubbed Hanna's file the Green Mystery Folder, and she watched her mother periodically drop in printouts, articles, and other various papers. Only once did Omani's curiosity get the best of her, and she went searching for the key, but never found it. The drawer remained locked, the mystery safe inside, until the day of her mother's funeral.

The reception, held at Omani and her mother's house, had been organized by Julia, her mother's life-long friend. It was a small gathering as Uncle Filip had insisted on only a limited number of people to attend. After the final guests left, Julia gathered paper plates and cups as sixteen-year-old Omani sat at the kitchen table frozen in grief. Her mother's closest friends and patients tried to comfort her, yet everything seemed like a dream. How could her mother be gone? Everything happened so fast— her getting sick and dying. Nothing made sense. Her eyes overflowed with tears and her shoulder's shook. "I miss her so much."

Julia hugged Hanna's daughter. "Me, too."

"Can I come live with you?"

"Only if your Uncle allows it."

Omani knew that would never happen. She loathed Uncle Filip. He was so bossy, always telling her what to do. At least there were only two years left before she obtained her maturity certificate. Then she could move away from him.

Filip came in the room and Julia approached him. "Would it be alright if I stayed here tonight with Omani?"

"You think I cannot handle a teenager?"

"It's been a difficult day for her."

Filip's in-ear device flashed blue. He waved his hand towards Julia. "Fine. You two can get this place cleaned up." He pressed a button on his ear-piece and walked away. "Glaus."

Omani fell asleep with Julia rubbing her back.

Late in the night Omani awoke to a loud bang and snuck downstairs to investigate. She hid underneath the steps and stared through the open slats into her mother's office.

Inside, Filip and two men tore the room apart. Using a hammer, one of the men smashed the lock on the drawer.

Omani bit her lip. *What were they doing? What did they want with her mother's stuff?* She wanted to protest, to confront them, but feared what they might do.

They loaded all the files into boxes, including the Green Mystery Folder that Omani was never able to look inside. She receded further back into the dark as the men exited the office carrying boxes. Hanna's computer protruded from a crate, wires hanging over the side. Filip followed them out, activating his ear-piece to make a call. "Liam? Meet me in an hour...Yes, I've got it."

She waited until vehicle doors slammed before emerging from her hiding place. *Why would Uncle Filip take everything? Who were those other men? And who was Liam?*

"Omani?" came Julia's voice, startling the girl. "What are you doing?"

"They took Momma's papers."

"I know."

"And her computer."

Julia put her hand on Omani's arm. "Okay, sweetie. Come back to bed."

"But those are Momma's things. Where did they take them?"

Filip would not get Omani's Mystery Folder. She looked at her meager collection of a couple dozen random documents, a few photographs, and some articles that couldn't be fully deciphered due to the printer running out of ink. Over the years she hadn't amassed much information. She began strong, but after getting caught by Elias, Filip's head of security, stuffing a paper in her shirt, she mostly gave up actively seeking out clues about her Uncle's work. Instead, she focused on her household duties and finding someone with whom to talk.

Her sparse findings were embarrassing compared to what her mother had gathered. Omani needed to do better. She must put her mind and actions back into gear to really find out what kind of schemes Filip was involved in. A part of her accepted it may be as he always claimed, working against terrorism, yet she wasn't totally convinced. And maybe, just maybe, someday she could find a way to leave the Compound and her Uncle's control. Omani slid the partial printout into her folder, not knowing if it held importance or not, and tucked her locked box away.

9

TREAZ

The next morning, skinny Danielle's teary green eyes returned and reality smacked Treaz again. This was definitely not just a bad dream. Her stomach growled. She prepared two pieces of toast, but they tasted wrong. Was it possible that foods tasted different to different people?

She affixed her gaze on the shifting eyes of the cat as the seconds passed...tick, tick, tick. It was kind of a cute clock. The unopened cardboard box remained on the unsteady kitchen table in this stranger's apartment. Suddenly, Grammie's words materialized in her head: "Search the boxes."

Had her grandmother been trying to tell her something? Her actions had been so bizarre. Is it conceivable that Grammie could have foreseen the predicament Treaz now was experiencing? Perhaps her words were some type of deathbed supernatural premonition? Could the contents of this box tell Treaz what she must do?

After a deep exhale, she removed the lid, and took out each of the box's items one at a time. First was a leather wallet she opened and examined. An Arizona driver's license showed a photo of whose body she currently inhabited. The name read Danielle Edwards with a birthdate putting Danielle at twenty-one.

At five foot, eleven inches she weighed a meager one hundred eighteen pounds. "Good lord, Danielle. You're way too skinny."

Next came a single credit card with Danielle's name, and a cheap flip phone. She didn't know they even made those antiquated devices anymore. No names showed in the contacts and there were no records of incoming or outgoing calls or texts. The date displayed confirmed to her again that now four days had passed since her birthday. While holding the phone, she tried dialing her own iPhone to see what might happen. After one ring, a recording came on stating no calls were being taken at that time and to try again later. Treaz shook her head. She couldn't recall Grammie's nursing home number as it had been in her speed dial, and she decided she must research and find it just in case she might garner enough courage to call. Who else could she contact? Her ex-boss? The one that terminated her employment for no reason? No. There was no one else to call. How pathetic.

Treaz retrieved a baggie with white pills like the ones Pearl Man had given to her to help with sleeping. And, a computer generated print out revealing a work schedule. Apparently Danielle worked at a Taco Bell nineteen hours a week. Lastly, she fished out a keyring from inside the box. It held a few keys, probably for the apartment door and mailbox, as well as a key to a Toyota.

She leaned back in her chair. Nothing in the box offered a hint of what she should be doing next. The throbbing in her head from yesterday had re-emerged and Treaz pressed on her temples. Danielle must own aspirin, so she went on an unsuccessful quest through every drawer and cupboard, but found no pain killers. She certainly didn't want to knock at her neighbor's door again, but at least now she had access to Danielle's car.

The security guard stood at the apartment office door as Treaz ventured down the steps and into the parking lot. She returned the wave and a smile. He didn't need to know anything further. Despite being a little nauseous about the situation, at least she wasn't breaking down in tears every ten minutes.

The parking spots were not assigned. She walked the pavement pushing the unlock button on the key fob until she spotted head lights flashing. The wish she held for the newest Toyota Prius model crumbled upon viewing the beat up, stripped down, 2008 Corolla. Great. She climbed in and the engine started with a sputter.

A ragged, paper map sat on the passenger seat. "Really?" She checked the cell, but neither GPS nor internet access came up leading to her suspicion that the phone didn't belong to Danielle but was one Pearl Man had purposely placed in that dumb box. Treaz would need to drive around to find the store.

After about ten minutes driving away from what appeared to be downtown Phoenix, she saw a Target. As she entered the store, the distinct smell of popcorn mixed with recently unpackaged product from China, assaulted her nose and she rubbed it. Treaz sensed her height as she towered over most other customers. Two women at a scarf rack stared at her as if she were a giant. They turned away and chuckled. Another young child pointed at Danielle before his mother shoved his arm down and whispered something to him. The uncomfortable sensation made Treaz very self-conscious, causing an involuntary slouch and gratefulness for selecting flat shoes.

One of the sale bins caught her attention and she stopped to peruse calendars with kitten photographs on the cover. What was she doing looking at cats, again? These were admittedly adorable.

Supplies piled up in her cart: aspirin, bagels, cream cheese with strawberries, low-fat milk, eggs, lunchmeat, and a few more items—including one of the irresistible cat calendars. She also bought a new toothbrush, because using a stranger's, epitomized disgusting. Not caring about the expense, Treaz justified Pearl Man could pay for whatever she needed or wanted! She couldn't navigate with an outdated map, so she picked out a GPS unit and deposited it in the cart.

After her shopping spree, she remembered about finding Grammie's nursing home number and used her GPS to locate a library. Locating an empty terminal, Treaz searched online for the facility. As she wrote down the phone number, she noticed the large, curly numbers she had made which was very different from Treaz's own small printing. It felt too flowery and she disliked it. She was uncertain if she would call Grammie that day. Although she badly wanted to hear her grandmother's voice, the way things were going, listening to news of Grammie's death would propel her over an emotional cliff.

Another idea—social media. A previous coworker coerced her to set up an account. She didn't interact with anyone online. She wasn't social. Treaz used an outdated photograph of herself for her profile picture, and she never made any posts. Occasionally, she would check if someone had miraculously sent her a friend request. Nobody ever did. Her only "friend" was that coworker who she hadn't seen or communicated with for years. Her timeline consisted of paid advertisements and dumb comments by the few people she had originally chosen to follow. Still, it might be a way to communicate with someone.

Surprisingly, she recalled her sign in information. Trying it she received the message:

The password you've entered is incorrect. Forgot password?

She tried again, same response. After each try, the information came back invalid. Did she want to

Create a new account?

Her hands began shaking. No. She did not. *I'm anti-social, remember? Nobody knows I'm here.*

Treaz burst into tears. Ugh! Not again. She had to get these emotions under control. The person to her left got up and hurried away, the one on her right pushed his headphones tighter over his ears, and another sitting opposite just kept sneaking peeks at her.

An elderly woman approached. "Are you alright? How can I help?"

Treaz shook her head. The kind woman offered to fetch some water, and Treaz accepted. "Thank you," she managed after drinking from the cone-shaped paper cup, and wiping her nose on her sleeve.

Upon arrival back at *home*, she swallowed the aspirin and unpacked her groceries. Everything seemed so exhausting. Her tongue resembled shag carpet and her breath bordered horrendous, so she fervently brushed her teeth. Back on the couch, she wondered again what she was supposed to do.

Not able to stand watching anymore afternoon television, Treaz began washing, drying, and putting all the dishes away. It felt better to be doing something productive. As she worked, she thought about the employment interview she went on several days earlier. Guess she won't be accepting that job. She had been unconventionally selected to do something else; exactly what remained a mystery. Treaz would be forced to interact with people, her least favorite type of work. Typically she performed back-office duties like accounting or data entry—anything that didn't require too much in-person contact. This would be different.

She spied a half-full laundry basket and figured the least she could do for adding a night in the psych ward on Danielle's medical record was to do her laundry. Treaz gathered up the rest of the dirty clothes spread around the apartment, removed the sheets, and retrieved the towels from the bathroom.

Carrying the overflowing basket, she took Danielle's keys and some change from the dish by the ticking cat, and exited. Using her foot, she tapped on the door directly across the hall. The same woman who had called security on her opened the door a crack and said nothing.

"Sorry about yesterday," Treaz apologized with a crooked smile. "Laundry room?"

"Down the stairs on the right," said the woman.

"Thank—" The door closed. "Stop being so friendly," Treaz muttered.

She sorted and started three loads at once. Twenty minutes into perusing a left-behind magazine on fishing, another tenant brought in her own pile of soiled clothes.

"Hi," said the girl with a tight smile. She looked to be of high school age.

"Hi," replied Treaz, feeling guilty for utilizing the majority of the machines. "Sorry, I had a lot to do."

The girl shrugged, put toddler outfits into the washer, and added soap. After dropping in the needed quarters, she sat down on the only open seat, next to Treaz.

Danielle must not know this girl, otherwise their greeting would have gone differently. The air grew uncomfortable. Should Treaz go wait outside? No, she'd try being pleasant. "Doing all the family wash, huh?"

The girl nodded but did not look up from her phone.

"My name's Treaz."

This got her attention. "That's a cool name."

"Thanks. It's a nickname my Grammie gave me."

"Mine's Christy. Those are my kid's clothes."

Treaz held back her surprise. "How many children do you have?"

"Three."

This girl, well, young woman, didn't look old enough to be responsible for three kids. She was still a kid herself. "Wow. You've got your hands full."

Without warning, Christy broke into sobs.

Inexperienced with this kind of outburst, Treaz's body stiffened as her eyes returned to the safety of the fishing magazine. When people cried at work, she'd just sneak away to the restroom or lunchroom. She'd find some reason to not deal with whatever the problem might be. Besides, it wasn't her business. Yet, she herself had wept uncontrollably many times after waking up in Danielle's body. How humiliating it was to lose it around other people, their reactions of pretending not to notice hurting even more. She awkwardly put her arm around the girl who turned to cry on her shoulder.

"Okay. It's okay," Treaz said, patting the stranger's back. Obviously, it wasn't *okay*. She recalled the nice elderly woman in the library who had tried to comfort her. "Christy, let me get you some water."

Christy sniffed and nodded.

"I'll be right back." Treaz walked to the door, then used Danielle's long legs to sprint to her apartment where she fetched a bottle and some tissue. She dashed back to the laundry facility, catching her breath before entering.

The girl wiped her face and drank several gulps of water, attempting to gain her composure. "Sorry for blubbering all over you."

"Naw. That's fine. I've had my share of moments lately."

Christy pushed a breath out through pursed lips. "My life's so messed up."

Hearing that sentiment, Treaz nodded her head in agreement. "Yeah, mine too." But she had already made the mistake of telling her story to Melody in the hospital and that hadn't turned out very well. She'd stick to listening. "You want to tell me what's going on?"

After Christy blew her nose again, she exhaled loudly. "You have kids?"

"No. Not even married," said Treaz.

"Yeah, well I'm not either. My boyfriend left two weeks ago. I can't go to work, because I have no one to watch my kids. Plus, daycare is too expensive for the kind of job I can do. The jerk got behind on our rent. At the end of this month, me and my girls are out, and it's almost Christmas."

"That's awful. Do you know where he is?"

Christy shook her head. "I can't take care of three little kids by myself. I had to pay a neighbor to watch them just so I could do my stupid laundry in peace."

"You shouldn't have to." Treaz wanted to say more about what a worthless piece of... No, focus on the girl. "Do you have someone else you can stay with? Like your parents?"

"They're divorced, and my mom doesn't even know about my babies."

Treaz sat up straighter. How was that even possible? "Christy, why haven't you told her about your children?"

Christy rubbed her upper arms. "She'd never forgive me now."

"How can you be sure unless you try asking?"

"She hated my boyfriend because he was nine years older than me. When I was fifteen, I just ran away."

Treaz scratched her head. If she had a fifteen year old daughter dating a twenty-four year old guy, she'd be upset too. "So, your mother has no idea where you are?"

"No."

"Oh, Christy. You need to call her. You need to call her now."

The tears began falling again. "She'll hate me."

Admittedly, not knowing Christy's family situation, the outcome may indeed be bad. "You have to try. I can't imagine she wouldn't want to see her grandchildren."

They talked until the laundry was done, folded, and back into each of their baskets. Treaz was reasonably sure she had convinced Christy to give her mother a call that night, but not one hundred percent.

"I'm in apartment 214. Come tell me what happened tomorrow, alright?"

Christy nodded. "You wanna maybe meet my girls in the morning?"

"Sure. That'd be fun." Treaz faked a smile, not wanting to admit she wouldn't know what to do or say around such young little humans.

Treaz put all Danielle's clean clothes away in drawers and the closet. The now sweet smelling towels were neatly rehung and the bed re-made. With nothing else to do, she found a vacuum cleaner and supplies under the kitchen sink, and went to town cleaning and scrubbing the entire apartment. Everything Treaz could straighten up, she did, thankful to be useful.

Sitting down to eat a turkey sandwich, she picked up the Taco Bell work schedule. Treaz had never worked in fast food, and was glad for one more day before needing to handle Danielle's job.

She stared at her new calendar affixed on the refrigerator by several feline magnets. December's photograph was a kitten that looked more like a wild leopard than a domesticated cat. It was beautiful. Treaz was baffled about why Danielle didn't have a kitty of her own.

After watching television for a bit, she popped two of the pills that Pearl Man had given her. She dozed off while praying she'd find the Asset Pearl Man had mentioned, do a good job, and be returned to her real life. Nobody knew she was missing except maybe Grammie—if she was still alive. And even so, her grandmother often would lose track of the time between Treaz's visits.

Treaz awoke in the throes of a deep coughing fit. She sat up, trying to catch her breath. After wiping her teary eyes, she realized she was naked. Looking around the room, the cat posters were gone and the bedroom completely different. "Oh God, not again," she said with a deep, husky voice.

10
OMANI

Omani bolted upright, her hair tousled, heart racing, and nightgown drenched with sweat. She switched on the lamp by the bed and looked at the clock. 11:02 pm. She'd gone to bed only an hour before. It had been decades since experiencing that old, reoccurring nightmare.

Her legs were tangled in something. Her progress down a dark alley was slow, like wading through syrup. The pounding footsteps of her Uncle Filip and Elias, closing in. Omani's heart raced as her pursuers gained ground. She dove behind a dumpster. With heavy breaths and perspiration dripping, she huddled close to the cold, blue metal.

"Omani. I will find you," her Uncle taunted. "You won't escape." The dumpster screeched as it moved to the side.

With nowhere to go, Omani shielded her eyes as if she could magically slip away. "Leave me alone!"

Elias scooped her up, draping her over his shoulder like a sack of potatoes. She kicked and slugged him in the back. Nothing deterred him.

Uncle Filip laughed at the spectacle. "You'll never run away from me."

"I hate you," she screamed.

What had triggered that horrific dream now? She assisted her legs and swung them over the bedside, tucked her crutches under her arms, and got to her feet. Moving to the window, Omani opened it a crack. The frigid night air blew against her face. She tried not to think about that horrid time in her life after which the nightmare ensued, but her mind would not release her from remembering.

A few months after Omani's mother had died, her Uncle purchased what he referred to as his Compound—a hundred acres, twenty miles from the Swiss Alps. They moved into the building which was half set up for personal quarters and the rest for his business. Omani was forced to live there. Although she desperately wanted the surgery on her legs that she'd been waiting for since a child and that her Uncle had promised to pay for, the thought of staying even one more year was unbearable. Certainly she could find a way to pay for her own medical expenses or find some charity to help.

The day was warm with a cool summer breeze. Seventeen-year-old Omani watched her Uncle Filip's car leave down the long, curvy road, away from the house. She hoped that would be the last time she ever saw him. For a month she had been making her plans. Now was her opportunity, and she hurried to the kitchen.

Ulrika was her timid, newly hired, private tutor, and Omani soon recognized she could talk her into just about anything—extra chocolate cake, a few tabloid magazines, and hopefully, a nice field trip to Lake Geneva.

"Please," Omani pleaded. "My mom used to take me there. I miss her."

Ulrika sighed. "You're not supposed to leave."

"My Uncle's gone for the afternoon. He'll never know. I want to go so badly. Water always makes me feel better. I've been so depressed." She put on her puppy eyes until Ulrika acquiesced. "I'll need to hide in the trunk of your car."

"But—" began Ulrika.

"It's fine. Let me get my stuff," Omani said passing by the woman. "We can't let anyone know. Drive around to the back by the kitchen."

Ten minutes later the trunk popped open. Omani tucked the chain from her pewter necklace in her shirt, then quickly tossed her crutches and backpack into the back of the small trunk. She sat down into the cramped space, and lifted her under-developed, weakened legs inside.

Ulrika gave a worrisome look at her tightly curled up student.

"Just tell the guards you're running an errand and you'll be back late," said Omani. She reached up and pulled the steel lid closed. She fought the immediate claustrophobic feeling by convincing herself she would soon be free of Uncle Filip, able to live her life where and how she wanted. Maybe she could even pursue a medical degree and establish a practice far, far away.

Omani and Ulrika spent the afternoon at Lake Geneva skipping stones and watching children splash at the waterline. The still, very cold water glistened a deep blue. Families and tourists snapped photographs and motioned at the golden eagle circling overhead.

It would be difficult to leave Switzerland, her home country, but Omani would not take the chance that Uncle Filip might find her. Inside her backpack were extra clothes, a blanket, and a little money she had squirreled away. Her idea was to lie low for a few days until her Uncle stopped looking for her, and then find a way to travel to America. Surely people would offer help to a young woman on crutches.

Ulrika went to buy them sandwiches and lemonade at a nearby vendor. Omani thought maybe now would be the time to disappear, but she convinced herself that she should stick with her original plan so nothing could go wrong. Soon enough, she would be long gone, or as far as she could manage on her own two feet plus walking aids.

After lunch Ulrika glanced at her watch. "I think we should head back."

"Aw, can't we stay a little longer?"

Ulrika folded her arms and shook her head.

Omani imagined Ulrika didn't want to get in trouble with her new employer. Yet, she knew for sure today would be the last day Ulrika worked for Uncle Filip. Lucky for her.

Ulrika opened the passenger door. "Here, sit in the front for now until we get nearer to your home."

As they traveled through one of the small towns, Omani peered at several of the places she had gone with her mother throughout her youth. The bakery had the best fresh doughnuts that melted into pure sugar as soon as they hit her tongue. The clothing store was where she had acquired special dresses for every birthday she could remember. "Stop," she shrieked.

Ulrika slammed on the brakes. "What's wrong?"

Omani pointed to a cheery window with yellow and blue checkered curtains, and a faded plastic sign of a sugar cone. "Let's get gelato!"

The woman caught her breath and laughed. "Oh. You scared me." She pulled over and parked. "That does sound good. We should hurry, though."

Omani got out of the car, slung the backpack over her shoulders, and crossed the street. This would be her only shot.

After her generous helping of dessert, she would complain of a stomach ache and excuse herself to the restroom. There was a rear door she had seen on many occasions that exited behind the building.

Once inside, the shop-keeper greeted her. "Omani. Lovely to see you. Where have you been?"

"Staying with my Uncle for now. But I hope to leave soon," she said, ignoring Ulrika's frown.

"Your usual?"

"Yes, but make it a triple scoop this time."

"Making up for lost time?" The woman served her large scoops of strawberry-cheesecake gelato on a sugar cone along with a bowl, just in case.

Ulrika ordered a single serving of vanilla. She sat across from Omani who had smears at the corners of her mouth from gulping down her icy delicacy.

Half-way through, a familiar voice came from behind. "Omani?"

Mid-lick, she turned to see Julia, her mother's best friend who had visited their home all during her childhood. Omani rested her cone in the bowl, stood, and as Julia attempted to hug her, Omani frowned and refused.

"I tried to find you, but you were gone," Julia said. "I wasn't sure where you went. How are you?"

Omani glared at her. "Why'd you push my mother into all that terrorist stuff?"

"What?"

"I know what you did. My Uncle told me," said Omani crossing her arms.

"We should go now," Ulrika said, rising to her feet.

Julia shook her head. "Your Uncle's a liar."

Omani held her ground. She may despise Uncle Filip, and couldn't wait to flee his household, but why would he make up lies about his own sister? "My mom was a good person and you ruined her."

Julia's eyes squinted and mouth turned down. "No, no, dear Omani. It isn't true."

"Then what were you doing?"

"I can't—"

"Come on. We need to go," said Ulrika taking Omani's crutches and holding them out.

Omani gave Julia a resentful snarl. "Did you ever even deliver that gift? Did you?"

The welcome bell jangled as the door burst open and two men entered. Omani recognized the mean, burly one as Elias. Her stomach churned, but not from the gelato. How had they found her?

Elias strode up, grabbed Omani's backpack, unzipped it, and pulled out a handful of clothes. "Planning a little vacation?" he asked, his voice full of sarcasm.

Ulrika covered her mouth.

Omani swiped for her bag. "Gimme my things."

He scattered everything on the floor, snatched the crutches from Ulrika, and shoved them into Omani's hands. "Let's go."

Julia grasped Omani's elbow. "I swear I didn't do anything. It was—"

Elias slapped Julia's face making Omani gasp. He gave the shop keeper a stern look making her disappear into the back office. Elias shoved both Julia and Ulrika into the arms of the other man who dragged them outside. Omani followed.

As the women were yanked across the street, Elias grabbed Omani's arm. "Hold on there. You're going with us." He strong-armed her into the back of a black sedan. "Keep her here. I'll be right back," he told the driver who engaged the automatic locks.

Omani could only observe from the darkened window.

Elias returned to Julia and Ulrika who remained under the strong restraint of the second man.

"Call the police! Get help," shouted Omani pounding on the window as a bystander hustled his wife and son away from the commotion.

The two men jostled the women into the back of another black car. Elias climbed in behind them while the other man got in the driver's seat.

Omani pressed her palms against the glass, the rage inside her growing. What were they doing?

After a few more moments, Elias got out and stomped back to instruct the driver. "Take her back."

"Yes sir."

"We're behind you in ten. Wait 'til I arrive."

"What'd you do?" bellowed Omani. Elias ignored her and walked away to get in Ulrika's car.

The engine of the vehicle Omani sat imprisoned in roared to life, and proceeded in the opposite direction from the trapped women.

Omani turned around and buried her head in her hands. What had she done? Why hadn't she left at the lake? Her Uncle would be so angry.

Back on the Compound, she sat before her Uncle's desk as Elias stood by the door.

Filip paced. "What were you thinking?"

"I just wanted to see the water," Omani lied. "My mom took me there when I had a normal life."

"I've warned you of the dangers. You are forbidden to leave here." Filip's phone toned, and he looked at it.

"What happened to Ulrika and Julia?" she demanded.

"Your tutor was appropriately reprimanded."

"She didn't do anything—"

"She took you—"

"It was my fault. I convinced her."

"Well…you should think about the consequences of your actions before you take them," he said.

She hadn't meant to get anyone in trouble, or fired, or…she didn't want to think of any other more severe outcomes. Omani stood. "What about Julia?" He consulted his phone again. "Uncle Filip. Where's Julia?"

He ran his hand through his hair. "You need to be punished."

She raised her hands. "Like living here with you isn't punishment enough?"

Filip scowled at her. "You're an ungrateful, untrustworthy child."

She'd never been ungrateful, but Uncle Filip had given her nothing to be grateful for. "That's bullshit."

He came from behind his desk and, without hesitation, struck her across the face. "I will not stand for such language in my house."

Shocked, she held her brightening, pink cheek, unable to speak.

"You will not have your surgery," Filip said smugly.

"What? You can't do that."

"I just did."

Omani's eyes flooded with tears. "But Uncle Filip. That isn't fair. I've been waiting my whole life. Please."

He nodded at Elias. "Take her to her room."

Elias stepped forward and Omani pushed him away.

"My mom promised—"

"Your mother's dead."

"Because of you!" she spat out at him.

Elias picked her up as she flailed and screamed at Filip. He carried her to her room where he dropped her on the bed. Omani sobbed. Her life was wrecked. How she hated her Uncle!

Omani's cheeks were ice-cold from the night air. She had not spoken to her Uncle for a long time after that day, but he had kept his word. She had never left the remote property since, and the corrective surgery on her legs had never happened. She still longed to leave his Compound in whatever manner possible; though now, she feared, it might be in a body bag. How would her life have been if she'd escaped from Uncle Filip? Where might she be living? What would she be doing? Would she have had a family of her own?

Omani recalled her fateful conversation with her Uncle six months following the finish of her last year of formal education.

"I want to be a doctor like my mother," said Omani to her Uncle. "I have to go to college for that."

Filip shook his head. "College is not for you."

Her stomach felt rock hard.

"It's too dangerous," said Filip. "I've told you many times, if anyone finds out you're here, your life will be threatened."

"I could change my name and go to America."

He shook his head. "Too risky."

Omani gritted her teeth. She had worked so hard to excel in her studies. "You can't stop me from going."

He gave her a tired expression. "I told your mother that I'd take care of you. I can't do that if you're not here."

"I can take care of myself."

"Really?" Filip came very close to Omani making her look at the floor. His voice grew louder as he taunted. She hated his taunts. "You have everything you need right here. Do you need something else? What do you need?"

"Can I at least take online courses?" she asked.

"No."

Omani's body began to tremble. "You're holding me prisoner."

Filip glared at her. "Basically, that's true. Thanks to your mother."

How her life had changed over the last three years—from the day her mother had died. "Well, then, I want to help stop terrorism, too." Only half believing that's what he was truly doing.

He returned to his desk and his paperwork.

"Come on, Uncle Filip," she protested. "I can't just do nothing." Omani waited for his response, determined not to leave until she got at least something she wanted. She walked closer, her eyes unable to avoid seeing her Uncle's favorite painting hung on the wall behind his desk. She never liked it nor understood why Filip revered it. Something, he said, about finding it in a basement on one of his many trips and it being key to his success. Omani couldn't imagine how the awful portrait of a raggedly-dressed man with sickly, bloodshot eyes, and an unshaven face symbolized anything positive.

Finally, he looked up from his papers. "You don't need to work. Many would enjoy that luxury."

Omani shouted, "This is no life of luxury. I have no friends. I have no freedom. I have no contact with the outside world. I have no purpose! This isn't a life at all. The least you can do is give me some meaning for my meager existence."

Filip sighed. "Alright, no need for such drama. I'll consider it." He left Omani blinking back tears. She tried not to cry in front of her Uncle because it infuriated him more. The man had no compassion, not even for his own niece.

A week later he approached while Omani ate breakfast. "I've found something for you to do." She lowered her fork and wiped her mouth. "I'm putting you in charge of all household and Compound duties."

She cast her eyes to the floor hoping for something a little more substantial, like tasks that would be important enough for her to travel off the confines of the Compound. Yet, Omani conceded. It was a job, at least, in which to begin.

"You'll be responsible for overseeing the grounds and building maintenance, kitchen staff, and housekeeping. You will work with the approved vendor for ordering house and business supplies." He folded his arms waiting for her reply.

"Will I have a say on how things are run around here?"

"Only in those areas."

Believing that Filip didn't have a sense of design or know how to maintain such a place, Omani saw potential for the building and grounds, and her mind immediately started thinking of improvements. Perhaps she would find at least some enjoyment in her imprisoned life spending Uncle Filip's money.

"You can start as soon as I have a computer set up for you. That'll be for keeping track of projects, doing inventory, and monitoring your budgets." Filip handed her a portable six by four inch device.

She had seen others using those pads and hid her excitement at receiving one of her own.

"You sync the device with your computer," Filip said. "I'll have IT show you how."

"I'll have internet access, right? I mean, I'll need that for buying things." She really hoped to get re-educated about the rest of the planet from the past two years, read the news, find an online friend or two, and maybe meet someone to take her on a date. Whoa. She'd better slow down. Uncle Filip would never go for that.

"No. You'll coordinate everything directly with the supplier when he comes."

Why did that not surprise her? She pushed down her anger, willing herself to be grateful. That was the most Filip had given her for a long time. Omani vowed to show him she could be successful and earn the opportunity for a more interesting job later on.

Another opportunity had never come from her Uncle and decades later she still did the same job. The only friendship, of sorts, she developed was with Mr. Bisch. Omani resigned herself to the fact that she would never do anything significant and important like her mother.

Securing the window, she retreated to the warmth of her bed. She scrunched her nose at the dusty wheelchair in the corner that Uncle Filip had purchased for her five years ago. *I'll never use you.* Yes, the chair would definitely be easier, but Omani refused to use it—solely because he wanted her to. If she could run it into the lake, she would. She managed to leave the apparatus in the corner, untouched, and was happy to let it remain a home for dust webs. She knew her mother Hanna would be livid that her own brother had refused to take Omani in for surgery.

Thinking about such things did nothing more than depress her. She pulled the soft down comforter around her neck, and rubbed the moisture from her eyes.

11

OMANI

Rafael came to Omani's room to repair her computer. He removed the control panel on the laptop as she hovered nearby. She had covert intentions.

"You have a family?" she asked.

"Just my dad and me," Rafael said. "My mother divorced him when I was a kid. We don't see her anymore."

"Sorry about that. My mom died when I was a teenager, so I don't see her either."

Rafael turned to her and smiled. "I hope not."

Omani chuckled. "Would you like some strawberry cheesecake gelato? I mean if it isn't too early in the day for you?"

Rafael looked at her. "It's never too early for gelato."

They both laughed and she dished them each a bowl from her secret stash.

After his first bite, Rafael "mmm'd" his approval. "Where'd you get the name, Omani? It's not common here in Switzerland."

"When my mother was traveling abroad as a child, she heard it and thought it was beautiful and mysterious. She vowed her future daughter, if she had one, would bear the name."

"It's very nice."

"Thank you." She stared into her bowl formulating her pitch. "I'm not very good at computers. I know you don't have time to teach me, but I wondered if you might bring me some books so I could learn on my own. I'd like to be more efficient at my job, especially at doing spreadsheets."

"The training's all online these days."

Omani nodded. "I don't have access to the internet."

"I heard about that when I was told to look into your computer issues." He shook his head. "I think that's pretty ridiculous."

She raised her hands. "I agree. What can I do?"

Rafael's phone toned, and he read the message. "I gotta go. I'll come back later to sync your tablet. Since it's so old, I have to do a special work around."

"My Uncle's only allowed a few upgrades over the years."

Rafael zipped up his small tool kit. "That thing's ancient. Probably belongs in a museum."

She picked up his empty bowl. "So, can you get me a book or two?"

"I'll see what I can find. That's the least I can do for some of the best dessert I've had in a while."

Omani laughed. "Oh, and don't tell anyone about the books or the gelato."

"You got it," he said. "I have some programming to do. Is around eight tonight too late to come finish things up?"

"That's fine."

When Omani returned to her room at 6:35 that evening, a plastic bag was set by her door. Inside were two old softcover books on computing. Some of the pages were dog-eared.

A knock came on Omani's door a few hours later. "Coming," she called out. She got up and stretched, her body stiff from reading non-stop since she had cracked open the first book.

"I'm sorry for being late," said Rafael. "You want me to come back tomorrow morning?"

"No problem. Come on in."

He entered the room and motioned to the two books lying on the bed. "You still need me or are you the expert now?"

"Thank you for finding them. I've learned so much already." The information was not only about spread sheets, but on several topics such as programming, server set-ups, and troubleshooting. All were complicated ideas she was confused by, but would attempt to master over time. Yet, Omani had another plan in mind.

They walked over to her desk, and she handed him her old tablet. Rafael prepared to sync the antiquated device to her laptop.

"Can you do that hacking thing?" she asked, keeping her face as innocent as possible. He looked warily at her. "I mean, the first book was talking about it, and I was curious on how it worked and if you could do it."

Rafael cocked his head. "Are you asking me to do something?"

"Oh, no. I'd never want to get you in trouble. But, I did wonder if you would set me up one of those server things."

"I don't think I'm supposed to do that, Omani."

"Would anyone find out?"

He focused back on his work.

Omani continued with her creative reasoning. "I think it'd really be helpful for me. I'd be able to find a way to save a ton of money. My stuff takes the lowest priority on the company servers, and things are always so slow. It's so frustrating. You should've seen Filip last week. He threw a fit because something he wanted wasn't ordered properly. He got so upset with me." She stopped rambling and waited for his reply.

He turned to face her. "You got any more gelato?"

She smiled. "Of course." She served them each a helping giving Rafael an extra scoop.

He swallowed his first bite. "I saw your Uncle's temper towards someone this afternoon. I don't want to lose my job after just getting it."

"And I would never want to jeopardize that," said Omani. "Perhaps you could do something separate from the company. Only you and I would know about it. Then I wouldn't have to learn how to hack."

Rafael snickered. "That's a talent in itself. What exactly do you think you can do with a private server?"

Nerves bubbled in Omani. "Find better deals for products on the internet. Learn how to fix things on my own. Maybe even earn a raise." Everything she just told Rafael was a lie. Making contact with the outside world to find a friend or two was the real goal, in addition to conducting her own research on her Uncle's activities. Omani would never receive a salary increase from Filip because he didn't pay her anything.

Rafael finished his work and handed her device back. "Thanks for the gelato." He began to leave, but stopped. "Got a personal question for you."

"Sure."

"How come you have to use the crutches?"

Omani exhaled. "Got in a bad car accident when I was really young. Crushed all the bones in my legs."

"Aren't there ways of fixing that?" Rafael pointed at her legs. "They've got robotic—"

"I know. I was supposed to get it when I turned eighteen." Rafael stared wide-eyed at her. Omani shrugged. "Good way to keep me here."

He nodded and left.

She sighed. Maybe he'd feel sorry enough for her to grant what she wanted. Omani read the computer books until midnight hoping at some point things would make more sense.

Omani worked all the following morning reorganizing the groundskeeper's storage space. Spring would be coming, and that meant new supplies would need to be ordered. True, Omani had months to make these decisions, but she liked being in the silent shed, by herself, thinking about things under her control like flowers, shrubs, and new equipment.

Later she sat in one of the smoking areas, gazing out to the mountains. The clear, blue sky looked summery, yet the frigid winter air kept her close to the heater. The building door opened and someone exited. Omani didn't turn to look, but heard a swipe then smelled a waft of smoke. She grimaced and reached for her crutches.

"I got something set up," came Rafael's voice.

Surprised, she turned. He leaned against a post. "I'll need to show you how to use it," he said. "Aren't you still having trouble syncing your device? I may have forgotten to do something." He winked at her.

Omani offered a half-smile and nodded. "In fact, I am. I'll submit a request right away."

Rafael stubbed out his cigarette in the receptacle and went back inside. Omani fought back a smile. She had been successful convincing him. She pulled out her device to enter a fabricated service request. Within a minute, she received a notification that someone would be by to address her issue.

At 6:15 pm that night, a knock came at her door, and she opened it.

Rafael grinned at her. "Hi."

"Hello." Omani motioned him in. "Thank you so much, Rafael. I didn't think you were going to come through."

"I'm addicted to sugar."

"Chocolate Chunk or Strawberry Cheesecake?"

"How about a lot of each?"

She laughed and dished him up a huge bowl of gelato.

Over the dessert, Rafael showed Omani how to access her private space. "Basically, you're using the same company server, because it's way faster. But I've written some code so everything's hidden. No one will know you're on it."

"You're so smart," said Omani, wanting to keep Rafael buttered up. "See, you DO have hacking skills."

He almost spit out a half-chewed chunk of chocolate. "You're so easy to impress. I wish I could impress my girlfriend like that."

"Oh, you have a girl?"

"Met her a couple months ago. Last night on the phone, we made it official."

"Congratulations. I hope she realizes how intelligent you are."

Rafael's cheeks reddened. He looked back to the monitor. "Just click in this lower right corner."

Omani craned her head closer. "I don't see anything."

"Ah, but therein lies the beauty." He clicked on the black screen, and a menu came up. Her mouth opened. It was the same one she had seen on the Comm's computer. Rafael pointed at the External selection. "Use this and ignore the rest."

"If I accidentally pushed another button, would anyone know? I mean, I don't want either of us getting caught."

"It won't do anything because, well, nothing will make any sense." He waved his hand. "Too complicated to explain."

Omani straightened her back, her curiosity piqued at the idea of endless exploring.

He selected External, and a bar came up. "Put in what you want to search for here and hit enter."

She looked at him. "That's it?"

He shrugged. "That's it."

"As a child, my mother always encouraged me with technology, but that was all nixed when I came to live with my Uncle. It's been awhile."

"Not much has changed." Rafael's phone rang, and he answered. "Yup? On my way." He hung up. "I gotta go throw gas on another fire. You think you can figure out the rest?"

"Yes, yes. And if I get stuck, I'm sure those books you gave me will help." He hurried through the remainder of his gelato and headed for the door. "Have fun."

"Oh, I will. We're obviously still good with keeping all this quiet, right?"

Rafael frowned. "Absolutely. I'm pretty sure Filip would kill me."

Omani nodded, knowing that Rafael's statement was truer than he could imagine.

Rafael walked away, and Omani's phone buzzed. It was a distressed Fritter, frantic that the incompetent cooks had prepared the wrong items for breakfast and that she wouldn't be ready for the morning meal.

"I'll be right there." Omani sighed. She needed to ease Fritter back from the ledge and would likely spend the next several hours in the kitchen. That meant having to wait before she could delve into the internet to try out her newfound freedom. Looking for whatever information she wanted, and talking to somebody online about anything, would do wonders for combatting her loneliness. Who cared about saving money on products since she only could work with Mr. Bisch anyway. She wanted to make a friend, a pen pal of sorts, like when her mother had introduced her to Franklin when she was a teenager.

12

TREAZ

Treaz jumped from bed, and bolted to the bathroom. How could this be? In the mirror looking back at her was not Treaz or Danielle, but another woman, maybe late-thirties, early-forties. Short, of average build, with light brown eyes. Her shoulder length hair was dyed multiple colors: orange, yellow, and blue. What happened?

Horrified, Treaz touched her new oily, broken-out face. She examined her naked body noticing an oval shaped scar on her left forearm. Running her fingertips over the surface, it was smooth and glossy, like from an old burn. Her fingernails were chewed close to the quick. Treaz broke into another coughing fit, her throat raw. She drank from the sink until the spasm died down. Staring at her face dripping with water, she couldn't believe it had happened again.

Pearl Man had lied. "I never should have trusted that man!" Her voice sounded raspy. Was this new woman a smoker? There were no cigarettes, lighters, or ashtrays in sight. However, the towels held a faint odor of smoke. She felt a pang in her gut; like when she thought about chocolate-covered raisins, and couldn't stop thinking about them until she consumed a carton. Perspiration formed on her forehead, and she found herself fidgety. Could she be craving a cigarette? She tried putting the woman in her place. "I despise smoking. Nasty habit."

At least, Treaz knew what to do. Once dressed, she checked out the rest of the apartment, glad that it wasn't a pig-sty like Danielle's place. The telling cardboard box on the kitchen table contained the bare basics—credit card, car keys, and driver's license. Her name was Bella Martin, thirty-seven, and still living in Phoenix. She half-hoped to find a pack of cigarettes just to satisfy her yearning, but there was none. Maybe Bella had quit recently—possibly right before Treaz showed up. The no-nonsense phone indicated the date as December 22nd. She dropped the cell to the table. Another couple days lost. The last item in the box was a schedule from a place called the Coffee Stop. Bella was due to work that afternoon.

Treaz hunted for some smokes. Nothing! "No smoking," she commanded herself. A dull pain in her ear throbbed, and she pushed her finger in and wiggled it, attaining no relief. Does this woman have an ear infection as well?

A knock came on the front door. She ignored it at first, but after it grew louder, she looked out the peep hole. *Excellent.* Exactly to whom she wanted to spew her angry words. Treaz opened the door and stood with her hand on her hip. "You lied to me."

Pearl Man tilted his head. "Nice hair." He entered and sat at the table. "Congratulations on finishing your first assignment."

Treaz raised her hands. "I didn't do anything. I never even found the Asset."

"It isn't always obvious. You know for sure when you Advance."

"Advance?"

"Once you do what you're supposed to, you're Advanced to your next Host body."

98

She clenched her jaw and strode closer. "You said I would get to go home."

Pearl Man shook his head. "I said you would return home after your final assignment."

Treaz leaned against the counter and crossed her arms tightly. "Why should I trust you? How do I even know my own body's safe to go home to?"

"It is."

"So how many assignments do I have to complete?"

He shrugged.

"Seriously?" She squeezed the sides of her head. That nicotine hankering returned with a vengeance, and she eased into the chair across from him. "I hate this job."

"Initial ones are typically pretty easy," Pearl Man said. "They aren't all like that."

She thought about Christy, the only person she had any real interaction with outside the hospital. "All I did was tell her to call her mother. I never had the chance to find out if she did or not. I need to find out what happened. And I promised to meet her daughters."

"It isn't your responsibility anymore."

"This is crazy," she said.

Pearl Man stood. "I think you're getting the hang of things. I'm running late."

Treaz slouched, unaware that her fingers pinched at a pimple on her chin, defeat in her voice. "Another problem employee?"

"Dentist appointment." He grimaced. "Don't pick those. It can leave scars."

She jerked her hand away, and shivered. Popping someone else's pimples? That's DISGUSTING.

The door closed behind Pearl Man—gone again.

How had she been chosen to do such an awful job? Surely something like this was illegal, let alone unethical, and impossible. She picked up the Coffee Stop paperwork which listed the phone number and address. Treaz called and asked for specific directions from Bella's place, doing her best impersonation of Grammie's shaky voice. The person giving the information remained cheery. Treaz hoped her boss and coworkers would be as patient with her.

The clock read 11:35 am. Bella better eat lunch and get ready for work. Not a good idea to be late on her first day. Actually, maybe she'd been working there for a year. She fought another urge for a cigarette to calm her frazzled nerves. Inside the refrigerator she spotted eggs and bacon. That would work for now.

In the bathroom drawer, Treaz located acne cream and carefully rubbed it on. After examining Bella's poor face, she was grateful she never had to deal with that affliction. She also found a much appreciated nicotine patch to help the almost debilitating compulsion. The instructions stated to adhere the bandage on the upper body. She chose her arm, seeing a small healing scratch on the inside—the same spot as on Danielle. Could that have something to do with the whole inhabiting the body of a stranger business? She coughed another painful round.

13

TREAZ

Treaz arrived to work thirty minutes ahead of her 2:00 pm start time to scrutinize the goings on from a distance. The Coffee Stop was an active establishment with a constant line of cars at the drive-thru and patrons arriving and leaving the retailer. How long had Bella worked there? Did she have friends, or a crappy boss? Treaz hoped she wasn't a barista because she didn't know how to prepare anything beyond a black coffee with a teaspoon of sugar. The unbearable need for a cigarette had thankfully subsided, leaving her to deal with the nervousness about walking into a job she supposedly understood but did not. She massaged around her ear, the pain coming and going.

At 1:55 pm she exited the safety of the vehicle and headed to the back entrance that employees had been using. She coached herself. "Just be low key. Pay attention to what others do. Don't mess things up for Bella." With a deep calming breath, she pulled open the metal door and entered.

The uniform question was resolved right away with the black pants and shirt plus a blue apron hanging from a hook with Bella's name posted above it. She ducked into the nearby staff bathroom and quickly changed. Following what others had done, she hung her street clothes back on the hook.

"Bella," came a voice that made Treaz jump. She turned to a young woman with a name tag that read Katie, Shift Lead. "Start with the restroom. A customer said it was almost out of toilet paper."

Treaz could handle that. She observed Katie approach a computer, find her name, and touch the Clock Out - Lunch button. Then she disappeared out the door. Treaz located Bella Martin on the screen and selected Clock In - Start Shift.

As expected, the place was as busy on the inside as the outside. None of the employees payed any attention to Treaz as they took orders, made specialty drinks, and cheerfully engaged with customers. She searched and found a small utility closet containing toilet tissue, and grabbed some rolls. Never had she considered doing that type of work, but she was grateful it wasn't anything more complicated.

Upon entering the first of two restrooms, she was appalled. Toilet paper lay all over the floor, water spots covered the mirror, the sink was clogged with hair, and the counter was soaked. How can people be so repugnant? She was afraid to look at the commode, yet she did. "Eww!" She hurried back to gather supplies including rubber gloves.

Treaz scrubbed and mopped. She noticed a chart on the wall where people logged cleaning for the last few weeks. Quite frequently Bella had her initials—B.M. Treaz chuckled. Appropriate letters. Apparently this needed to be done every hour. She set her phone timer so she could stay on schedule. When she returned sixty minutes later, everything looked worse than the first time.

Katie passed without stopping. "Trash on the patio's overflowing and there's fingerprints on the display cabinets."

As she worked, Treaz tried to figure out who the Asset might be. Would it be an employee or a customer? The delivery guy or the man that came to fix the plumbing? Might it be Katie? What an inefficient way of running a business.

Treaz hauled several loads of garbage to the dumpster behind the store passing by two other employees who were mired in smoke. She was half tempted to join them and give Bella a break, but Treaz had been doing so good for her Host's body. Plus, she didn't even know HOW to smoke a cigarette. No, she would not promote the habit. Smiling at her coworkers, they ignored her. Perhaps like Treaz, Bella was more of a loner.

While Treaz collected the trash in the tight back office, Katie got up from the computer and exited leaving a good opportunity to jump online and find out Grammie's nursing home number again. She had to commit that to memory. It only took her a few seconds to find and make a note of it. When she stood up, she turned right into Katie watching her.

"Bella. You know the rules. Nothing personal."

"I'm sorry. I just needed to look up a number."

"That's what your phone's for. The shelves need restocked."

She apologized again and hurried out. *If only Pearl Man provided a decent phone with internet service.*

Treaz buzzed around finding eaves-dropping and watching the customers quite fascinating. Some would sit in the same spot without moving, absorbed in their laptops. A few enjoyed e-readers and paperbacks. Couples sat gazing into each other's eyes and playing footsie under the table. Others sipped lattes, not looking up from their phones. The stays were from five minutes to several hours.

During the evening, an obese man in his early twenties sat down awkwardly, his eyes beady against his heavy face. A thin woman, perhaps his mother, went to purchase a donut and chocolate scone and put it in front of him without saying anything. She chose another table at which to sit and wait. After he had devoured the food, he pulled a small pad from his pocket and furiously scribbled notes on yellow paper. When Mom saw his treats were gone, she went to buy more. A few minutes later she delivered him a croissant and over-sized blueberry muffin, then once again went to her own table without communication, or consuming anything herself.

Treaz found this parent-child interaction quite disturbing. A mother was being forced to cater to her lazy son. The young man needed some serious discipline. He ate every fat-laden dessert she provided, and they never spoke to each other. Sad. Crumbs gathered in the man's scruffy beard, on his shirt, and dropped to the floor around him. More for her to sweep. The same routine continued for at least ninety minutes. As the odd pair left, the guy ripped out the pages he wrote, balled them up, and discarded them in the garbage.

On the way home from work, she stopped to purchase throat lozenges, to ask a pharmacist about alleviating ear discomfort, and to eat a greasy fast food dinner. It was too late to call Grammie, so she popped a couple sleeping pills, and lay with a warm compress against her ear.

The day appeared to have been a waste of time since she'd only interacted with Katie. Treaz half-hoped she would be Advanced again, as Pearl Man had explained, so she didn't need to be a thankless janitor. But, the next morning, she awoke again as Bella. She lay in bed trying to make sense of things, but the powerful urge to smoke prompted her to get out of bed and apply a new nicotine patch.

The second day on the job at the Coffee Stop progressed as the first did—scrubbing, cleaning, restocking, mopping. When Pearl Man showed again, she would complain.

As Treaz wiped down one of the machines, her forearm knocked over a cup of steaming milky espresso sitting on the counter without a lid. She quickly moved her arm as the scalding contents almost spilled in the same spot where Bella's original burn scar was located. Treaz figured she'd been working at the retailer for a long while.

She wondered why people placed used cups and soiled napkins next to the receptacles as opposed to taking the extra quarter second to drop them in. They left food remnants, empty wrappers, and drink spills. People carelessly picked up sale items, then shoved them back on the wrong shelves. All the same things she did as a customer, never thinking twice about the person having to tidy up her mess.

Around the similar time as the night before, the three hundred pound young man and his mother were back. They repeated the identical routine—her continuously delivering him food, no communication, and him scribbling. It was almost creepy to witness. Once again, when they headed out the door, his yellow papers were discarded. Curious, Treaz went to remove the garbage bag, saw the ball of papers, and slipped them in her pocket.

After her shift, she uncurled his scribbling while sitting in her car. It appeared to be computer code or technical notes for the design of something. Math equations penned on some pages, sketches on others. Why would he throw such detailed work away?

Before she went to bed, Treaz straightened Bella's apartment —hanging clothes, clearing out the refrigerator, vacuuming the carpet, scrubbing the bathroom. She chuckled. Perhaps she was taking her day job too seriously. Honestly, chaos was like an unreachable back itch. Having something crooked or out of place knocked her attention away from where it should be. Multiple cooked meals had been burned because of her need to declutter or organize or clean.

She moved the toaster oven to wipe underneath and found a small card amongst the dust. It was a doctor's appointment reminder for three weeks ago. Had her Host gone? The line for a patient name had been left blank, so it may have been for someone else, though, Bella didn't seem to have any friends. No one acknowledged her at work or ever came to her apartment door. Treaz tossed it in the trash and finished her housekeeping.

14

OMANI

Omani slipped a stick of peppermint gum in her mouth as she worked at the table in her living quarters. That simple action still reminded her of being twelve and getting reprimanded for chewing gum by her foreign language tutor.

Mrs. Schneider delivered a passionate explanation as to why it was such a horrible offense. "Omani. Everything you've eaten today, scrambled eggs, carrot chunks, cookie crumbs and pieces of fish, all have been absorbed into that sticky mess that you insist on chewing on all afternoon. It is a repulsive and unsanitary habit."

Grimacing and chuckling simultaneously, Omani pictured the unsavory visual as she assembled packages with information about the Compound amenities—dining room and workout facility hours, do's and don'ts for the living areas, and a complete map of the complex. Filip had hired a lot of new staff lately, and she attached clips to seven new employee badges. She assigned sleeping rooms and put in requests for housekeeping to get them prepared. Even though Uncle Filip thought she did too much for the new employees, he gave her thirty minutes to orient the eager men and women.

If it were up to Filip, he'd probably opt instead to give a fifteen minute lesson on how to ignore Omani. Most people would start off the first few days being friendly, but then would be schooled by Filip or some other senior person that she was to be avoided unless there was a facility or housekeeping issue. She thought back to when she was barely twenty-one, bored, and starved for human interaction.

Omani had taken a walk into the garden in search of Stefano, a charming eighteen year old grounds boy employed by her Uncle. He was an olive-skinned Southern Italian who spoke of the vineyards of Italy. Stefano always set her heart fluttering when he looked over and gave an abandoned smile. As with the other workers, he lived on the Compound and, when he left for his five days, they were the longest ones of the month for Omani.

Stefano acted interested in her, despite her crutches and her endless barrage of questions about life away from the confines of the property. "It's too bad you can't come with me on my time off next week," he offered as she sat watching him turn dirt over in a flower bed.

"My crazy Uncle would never allow it," said Omani.

"Well, you're an adult. Can't you make that decision?"

Omani cast her eyes to the yellow and purple pansies he was planting. "I'd like to think so, but—"

She stopped talking when Stefano sat down on the grass, really close. As their shoulders and thighs touched, perspiration formed on her forehead and under her arms. He rubbed his hands together, and Omani saw the mixture of soil and fertilizer fall away. A faint scent of man-sweat emanated from his shirt. She had smelled man-sweat before from the maintenance guys and her Uncle when he passed by after lifting weights, but those male odors were gross. This boy smelled sweet.

Stefano stroked her cheek with his fingers. Her whole body shivered at his touch, and her face flushed. This was the closest she had been to a boy since age thirteen when one kissed her behind the school bleachers—a terrible, hard kiss where he thrust his tongue deep in her mouth, making her gag.

But, Stefano was different. He placed his hand behind her neck and eased her slightly forward to meet his suntanned face. The roughness of his chapped lips were easily ignored for the gentleness of his kiss—nothing pushy or harsh or hurried. Omani held her breath and closed her eyes, hoping he couldn't feel the pounding of her heart. That was what she imagined a kiss was meant to be like, and she didn't want it to stop.

"What's going on here?" came Uncle Filip's booming voice.

Omani jerked away as Stefano jumped to his feet. "Mr. Glaus," he stammered.

Filip stepped up to the boy, who was six inches shorter and twenty pounds lighter. "Is this what I'm paying you for? To take advantage of my niece?"

"No sir."

"Uncle Filip," Omani said getting up and positioning her crutches. She had seen her Uncle's brutal temper more often than she'd liked. "It wasn't his fault."

"I understand all too well about young men," said Filip grabbing Stefano by the collar.

Tears flooded her eyes as she yanked on Filip's arm. "It was me. I asked him to do it. Please, don't hurt him."

He shoved Omani down on the freshly planted flowers, then gave Stefano a solid punch to the face without releasing his grip. Blood flowed from Stefano's nose.

"Please, Uncle Filip. Stop!" pleaded Omani. He dragged Stefano across the grass and into the guard shack. She couldn't hear what was happening, but a few minutes later, one of the guards came out buttoning his sleeves. He got into one of the trucks while the other guard carried out Stefano's limp body and tossed it in the back. The gate opened, and they drove away as her Uncle walked back to her.

"Oh no, no," Omani wailed. Her heart shattered into a million pieces. "I hate you," she screamed at him.

Filip raised his fist making her cower. He shoved his finger near her face. "Omani. Never again."

"I wanna leave this horrible place. I wanna life. I wanna go to school and have a career. I wanna get married and have babies."

"That will never, ever happen. Never," he said. "I would hunt you down and make you very, very sorry."

Omani brushed off one of the new hire packets where an escaped tear had fallen. She never found out if Stefano survived and made it back to his beloved Italy.

Having grown used to the loneliness over the years, she still attempted to interact with people—especially if she had specific intentions. Every hellish anniversary of Hanna's death, Omani did something she imagined her mother would have done. One time, in honor of the many bowls of gelato she and her mother had shared, Omani requested Mr. Bisch install a custom made chest of drawers in her room. All the drawers appeared uniform from the front, but the bottom drawer was a freezer where she stored her gelato stash.

Omani opened her secret freezer and removed a half-eaten carton of strawberry cheesecake, her favorite. She thought about a request she made another year on the commemoration day.

Omani cornered a timid gentleman who had worked in Research for three years. After observing his lack of interactions with other employees, she determined he would be safe enough to ask. "Good morning, Tomas."

"Hello," he replied, his eyes staring anywhere but at her.

"I need a favor."

He looked around to see if anyone was watching. "A favor?"

"Yes. Today is a special day for me."

Tomas glanced up. "Is it your birthday?"

"No. It's the anniversary of my mother's death." His cheeks reddened. "I need you to do something." Again, Tomas surveyed the area. "I know you're not supposed to do stuff for me, but this isn't a big deal." She moved closer. "My mom passed away when I was just a kid. Since you're in research, could you find out what her work was? I mean, she was a doctor, but she did other things too." Tomas shifted his feet. "Please, Tomas. It would mean so much. I promise not to tell anyone."

After a few moments, Tomas nodded. "I'll see what I can find."

"Thank you. I'll be in the kitchen most of the day."

At lunchtime, Tomas entered the kitchen where Omani sat studying blueprints for a pantry remodel. He dropped an envelope on the table, then exited without a word. Her heart sped with the thought of reading more about her mother's work beyond her physician duties; all those hours spent on the computer gathering things for her Green Mystery Folder. Omani's gut rumbled as she unfolded three pages, although she had wanted more. The information highlighted Hanna's medical work, but nothing further. The disappointment hit Omani hard. She so desperately needed to prove to herself that her mother had not been involved in anything bad, like Filip always suggested. She tucked the papers away. Even if Hanna commiserated with terrorists, never could Omani love her any less. She was her mother.

The next day, Uncle Filip summoned Omani to his office. "Sit down," he told her.

"I'm fine," she said, not wanting to stay around him for long.

He stared at her with piercing eyes until she finally sat down. "I had to fire Tomas this morning."

A wave of nausea came over Omani. Had Tomas said something or had someone seen him researching or giving her the papers? "Why?"

He shook his head. "You already know what happened to your mother. You were there. She got sick and died."

Her fists clenched. "I just—"

"Why do you keep trying to make more of it?"

Omani tried unsuccessfully to hold her anger. "I could have looked it up for myself if you'd give me access."

"We can't take that chance."

She stood. "What is it about your business that's so secretive?"

Filip's chair squeaked as he leaned back. "I've told you a thousand times. We fight international terrorism. Because of me, cities and lives are being saved."

Omani wanted to believe him so badly, but she could not be totally sure.

"Your mother's the reason why we do what we do. You can thank her." Her blood boiled. He was always blaming her mother. Filip slammed his palms on his desk. "Just do your job, or I'll hire someone else to do it, and you can go back to doing nothing."

"What'd you do to Tomas?"

"Stay out of it."

Omani sighed, popped the lid off the gelato container, and used a tablespoon kept just for that treat—that comforting, yet temporary little taste of heaven. The luscious dessert melted slowly in her mouth and slipped down her throat helping her to forget her depressing life. "Savor," she remembered her mother's nudging.

15

TREAZ

Treaz woke once more with a sore throat and a hacking cough, so she dragged herself out of bed and found tea bags in the cupboard hoping the hot liquid would sooth everything before her planned call. As she sat sipping the tea, she decided that Bella must have started smoking at a young age since she already had the dreaded smoker's voice. When she felt sufficiently calm, Treaz dialed the number to Grammie's nursing home.

She did not recognize the cheery woman that answered the phone. "Creighton Elder Care. How may I help you?"

"Elena Popa's room, please."

"And the security code?"

This was not something Treaz would forget no matter whose body she occupied. She had established it when moving her grandmother into the facility. "Ten seventeen." It was Treaz's mother's birthday.

A faint tapping came as the receptionist entered the information. "Thanks. I'll connect you."

A warmth engulfed Treaz. She was about to talk to the one remaining person in the world who loved her. At least now she knew Grammie had not died, not yet. It rang several times, which wasn't unusual. On the eighth ring, Treaz heard the familiar rustling and fumbling, then that beloved, sweet voice. "Hello?"

She stood, her hands trembling. "Hi Grammie. It's Treaz. Oh my God, it's so good to hear your voice. I've missed you so much."

"Who?"

"Your granddaughter."

A few moments passed. "This isn't my granddaughter."

Treaz walked from one side of the room to the other. One hand gripping the phone, the other motioning wildly. "No, it is, Grammie. I just caught this really bad cold and—"

"Why are you calling me? This is not Treaz," said Grammie, her voice agitated.

"It is. I'm so sorry I haven't been able to visit—"

Her grandmother's voice shook as she yelled. "What have you done with my Treaz?"

She sat down hard on the kitchen chair agonizing over the old lady's worried tone. "I swear it's me. I'm fine."

"No. You better not—" Grammie's voice trailed away as the phone was taken from her. Treaz recognized the voice of the person trying to settle her grandmother.

"Alright, Elena. Calm down," said Barbara, her long-time caregiver. "I'll handle it."

"Where's Treaz? That isn't her," cried Elena.

Treaz rubbed her forehead, hating that Grammie was so upset.

"It'll be fine. I'll find out," Barbara reassured. Then she spoke into the receiver. "Who is this?"

"Hey Barbara, this is Treaz."

The woman was sharp and assured. "You sound nothing like her."

Treaz sprung back to her feet. "I told Grammie, I've got this terrible cold. This is Treaz, Nadia Popa, Elena's granddaughter."

"I'm not sure who you are, but calling to disturb a frail woman is heartless. What is wrong with you?"

"No, no, please, Barbara," Treaz pleaded. "I realize I sound completely different. The code is ten seventeen."

"How'd you get that number?"

Treaz's desperation came out as anger. "Because I'm the one who set it up."

Her heart broke as Grammie ranted in the background. "Where's my granddaughter, Barbara? Where?"

"Whoever you are, don't call here again or I will call the police," said Barbara. The phone slammed down.

Treaz broke into a coughing fit and bile erupted in her throat. She had to quiet her emotions otherwise there would be no way to prove who she really was. Taking several deep breaths, she swallowed aspirin for the throbbing in her head, and she tried again.

The same receptionist picked up. "Creighton Elder Care. How may I help you?"

She put a smile on her face, trying to soften her voice and sound upbeat. "Yes, Elena Popa. The code's ten seventeen."

After a pause, the woman apologized. "I'm sorry. That code is not valid."

"I just called five minutes ago, and it worked. It's one zero one seven. Will you please check again?"

"Please hold."

Treaz nervously picked at a pimple on her neck as a scratchy version of Frank Sinatra's *My Way* played on the phone.

The receptionist returned. "That code is no longer valid."

"I put my grandmother with you people over ten years ago. She's in the third room on the left. Her primary caretaker is Barbara and—"

"Sorry, but you need the correct security code."

"I have the right damn code!"

The woman's cool demeanor never wavered. "If you'd like to establish a new one, you'll need to come into our office with proper identification."

"What? That's ridiculous. I'm out of town."

"Until you come in, please don't call back again. Otherwise, we'll report your harassment to law enforcement." The call disconnected.

Numbness spread through Treaz's body, like getting a dozen shots of local anesthesia all at one time. Those moronic caregivers acted so unreasonable. If they'd just given her a chance to explain. Grammie sounded so confused. She needed to figure out a way to get back to San Antonio to see her. Maybe when she got a few days off, she'd use Bella's credit card to book a trip since the drive would take too long. Treaz's gut told her she could convince Grammie of who she was no matter what she looked like, but getting past the staff would be more difficult as she didn't look anything like herself or possess any identification. Treaz would make it work even if she had to sneak in an open window.

A woman touched Treaz's shoulder while she was emptying the patio trash at the Coffee Stop. "Excuse me?" Treaz turned. "I think we may have met before. My name's Yolanda."

Uh-oh. Treaz was uncertain how to play the question. "I'm not sure. My name is Bella."

Yolanda frowned. "That's a pretty name. I don't think I'd forget that. Were you at a dental conference last year?"

Chances were slim since Bella worked at a coffee shop. "No. Not me." Then the thought struck her—maybe this was her Asset. She hadn't known Christy had been one the first time around. Treaz had to keep Yolanda engaged in conversation until she figured out how to help—perhaps she needed to call her mother too. "Are you in the dental field?"

"Sometimes. I change jobs a lot. At that time, I was a receptionist in a dentist office."

Interesting. "Do you get bored easy?"

Yolanda thought for a few moments. "You might say that."

Treaz tied up the garbage and secured a new bag. "Well, variety's good."

The woman went on to describe holding more positions over the past three years than Treaz thought possible. Her resume must be five pages long. As she continued talking, Treaz realized that maybe Yolanda was not an Asset at all, but another Transitioner, like herself. The fact that she changed employers so frequently totally made sense. The woman was a talker, barely taking a breath. Katie, the shift lead, squinted as she walked by, and Treaz worried that Bella might get in trouble again for breaking a rule. Unsure how to broach the topic, she finally interrupted. "Yolanda, are you a Transitioner?"

"A what?"

Treaz spoke matter-of-factly because she either was or she wasn't. "A Transitioner. Someone who takes over somebody else's body to try and accomplish something?"

Yolanda stammered, "Uh. I've tried lots of different things. But—"

Treaz leaned in, lowering her voice. "You can tell me. Isn't it wild that Pearl Man's company has the technology to even do this body switching thing?"

The woman's eyes grew wide. "That sounds sort of unusual."

"Do you know anything else about how long we have to do this?"

"I think I was mistaken," Yolanda said.

Before Treaz could do or say anything further, Yolanda bolted out the door. Nope, not a Transitioner. She smiled knowing she had at least found a way to stop that woman from talking.

After the evening rush, Treaz cleaned the filthy glass doors. Why don't people actually use the door handle?

An older sedan pulled into a parking spot, and out climbed that same mother and her massive offspring. It took him some time to get out, hike up his pants, and walk to the door that Treaz held open for them. The mom entered without so much as a smile, but her son nodded in acknowledgement. They fell into their same routine of her fetching him food, yet choosing to occupy a table away from him and not eating or drinking anything herself. So weird.

Twenty minutes later, as Treaz scrubbed hardened jelly from a chair, the mother walked to the counter, no doubt to purchase more goodies. Treaz took the opportunity and went to wipe the table next to the guy. "Hello," she said.

He looked up from his writing. "Hi."

She pointed at the empty food wrappers. "I can take that if you'd like." Treaz grinned as she scooped up the plastic wrap. "Don't you just love those french-almond macaroons? They're my favorite," although she had never tasted them. He nodded. "I see you in here a lot. My name is Treaz."

He gazed at her name tag. "It says, Bella."

Oops. "Yes, but I go by Treaz. What's your name?"

"B.S."

"Like in…?"

He grimaced and dipped his head. "Leave it to my loving father."

Treaz felt sorry for the guy. "What's your real name?"

118

He sighed. "I don't know what's worse, Beckman or B.S. Who cares anyway?"

"I like Beckman. It's a very distinguished name."

He looked up and smiled, but it soon faded, his eyes dropping. Treaz sensed someone behind her and turned to face the mother.

She held a raspberry streusel bar and a mug of hot chocolate. "Why are you speaking to my son?" Her voice icy enough to freeze the drink.

"Only saying hello," said Treaz politely.

The mother set down his food. "He doesn't like talking to people."

Beckman shook his head, grinding his teeth.

Treaz bowed her head slightly and walked away, her insides fuming. *What a witch.* She decided to make Beckman her Asset, whether Pearl Man liked it or not. Every person needed someone to recognize them, not shun or ignore them.

The next day was December 24th. The Coffee Stop bustled with patrons buying gift cards and downing caffeine and sugar-laden drinks to propel them through their last minute shopping obligations. Some were laughing and celebratory, but many impatient and grouchy.

Beckman and his mother came in two hours before their normal time due to the shop closing early for the holiday. During his mother's trip to the cashier, Treaz walked by to greet him. "How's it going, Beckman?"

"Alright."

She glanced to the front seeing his mom was being served. "You ready for Christmas?"

He shrugged. "I guess."

"You have family coming to town?"

"Naw. It'll just be me and my mom. Oh joy. How about you?"

Nice—he asked about her. "My grandmother can't travel, but I'll go see her soon." She saw Beckman's mother making her way through the crowd, balancing his nightly input of sweets. "Well, I hope you have a nice day."

"Thanks. You too."

She hurried away before his mother arrived.

Upon exiting the shop, Beckman trashed all his notes and raised his hand to wave goodbye to Treaz. He wasn't a lazy monster, as she had initially assumed, but just a shy, lonely young man with an over-dominant parent.

Treaz braved the hectic grocery store to buy a pre-made turkey dinner for her day off. She was looking forward to doing nothing but distracting herself with old movies. Maybe she could go find out if Danielle was back in her own body now. Or visit Christy to meet her kids. She inhaled deeply. What a mess.

She slept in late. Her earache was back, so she applied the warm compress again. The meal from the store re-heated rather well. While doing the dishes, she spotted a stubby gold key which likely went to a mail box that she had not bothered to check the entire time since being in her Host's body. Thinking a short walk would do her over-filled belly good, she went to collect the mail. The day was gorgeous at a comfortable mid-sixties, and Treaz walked around the complex observing people carrying bags of presents and containers of food. Kids played in the green area with new bicycles and baseball mitts. Everybody with family—everybody but her…and Bella.

There was the typical over-abundance of sales advertisements, an invitation to a Christmas Eve service at a local church, and an electric bill. Also, a thin envelope from a doctor's office—the same one that was listed on that reminder card she had found. She held the envelope up to the light trying to determine what was inside—an invoice or a receipt? Having no idea how long she would be living in Bella's body, when she returned to the apartment, Treaz slid a kitchen knife under the flap and removed a single page that stated everything she needed to know.

Bella had been diagnosed with stage two cancer of the larynx. Her doctor shared concerns about her missing her last appointment, and his office manager's inability to reach her on the phone. He insisted that she call immediately to reschedule so they could conduct follow up tests and discuss treatment options.

Treaz sat down in the nearest chair. "Good God, Bella." No wonder the lozenges didn't help the burning in her throat. She cupped her face in her hands. Had Treaz taking over her body caused her to miss the appointment? No. She hadn't been Bella that long. Her Host was obviously ignoring the problem. The poor woman must be dealing with this by herself, keeping it a secret from anyone at her job. Where was her family or friends? If any, they were probably leaving messages on her real cell phone, wherever it was being kept.

What would happen if Bella's body died? Would that mean Treaz would die as well or would she go back into her own body? Where was her own body being kept? In her bed at home? In some hospital somewhere? Was someone else being hosted in her body? There were so many things she didn't understand about her crazy predicament. One thing she absolutely did not want to happen was to die in Bella's body. Undergoing any medical procedure made her queasy, yet the idea of dying in another person's body sounded horrific, so as long as she occupied Bella's body, she would do whatever she could to care for it. Treaz would call after the weekend to schedule a doctor's appointment. An even better plan was attempting to find her Asset, finish her assignment, and get out of that Host body fast.

16
OMANI

The entire next day at work, Omani's mood reflected her excitement for her upcoming evening activities. She even bid Uncle Filip, "good morning," when she passed him in the hall. It didn't matter that he completely ignored her greeting. How her luck had changed, and the anticipation of going on the internet kept her smiling. Rafael was so nice to set everything up for her.

That night she hesitated before beginning her computer work. Would Uncle Filip know? No. She trusted Rafael. He didn't want to get caught either. After a long exhale, she moved her curser to the corner of the dark black screen. From the first time Omani clicked on External on the menu she became hooked. She found everything and anything interesting as she'd missed so much being away from the world beyond her Uncle's Compound.

The websites, videos, articles, news and gossip were all fascinating. Many writers didn't hold back. They said whatever they wanted and posted every kind of photograph and video she could imagine, including some she didn't want to imagine. Those were quite disturbing at times, and she'd quickly go on to something else.

A ticker tape of constantly changing advertisements crept along all sides of the screen. It appeared that people were free to order as they pleased—recreational marijuana, house-calling prostitutes, online gambling. Headlines flashed demanding her attention—the latest scandal in the government, the infidelity of a famous actor, images from a holographic concert of a deceased musical artist, a reporting of yet another black hole.

"I've missed a lot," Omani murmured.

After realizing the clock read 10:30 pm, she shook her head at how the hours had flown by. She needed to be more careful and not waste so much time on unimportant things. One reason she wanted access was to conduct her own research and not rely on anyone else to find information for her.

Omani typed her mother's name in the search bar—Hanna LaZarres. She hunted through several names and results before finally finding two mentions of Hanna. The first was the same article as Tomas, the previous Researcher of her Uncle's, provided to her years ago at the expense of his job. The second link led to a very brief obituary Omani had never read.

Dr. H. LaZarres, 35, recently died from an undisclosed illness. Dr. LaZarres was not married. Funeral services will be private and held at the convenience of the family.

Omani clenched her teeth at the insufficient description of Hanna's life, for all her career accomplishments, and work in the community. And her own daughter, Omani, was never mentioned. Filip must have been responsible for writing the meager acknowledgment.

She always suspected he withheld the real reason for her mother's death because he had something to do with it.

Next, she searched for Julia Bracker, her mom's best friend. Aside from details on the company Julia worked for, only a single short mention showed up in a local newspaper.

Chief Executive Officer of Milfi Advertising, Julia Bracker, has resigned her post without explanation. The company's spokesperson stated that Mrs. Bracker no longer lived in the area and remained unavailable for comment.

Omani sighed and entered Filip Glaus.

Several posts and articles popped up, and she scanned through some of them. All highlighted his proclaimed success in fighting against terrorism across Europe and the United States. One offered Filip's standard response.

When asked about his counter-terrorism efforts, Mr. Glaus, a man known for his few words, was quoted as saying, "For security reasons, I cannot go into any details, but my organization is saving thousands of lives and millions of dollars in property by utilizing the highest of covert technologies to combat terrorism."

Could that really be true? Omani stretched out her stiff arms, yawning deeply. There was one last person to search for and she leaned forward. She typed—Stefano, then she stopped. Omani never even knew the surname of the young man that easily could have stolen her heart. Her eyes watered and she turned off her computer. She had learned nothing new and her investigation of the people closest to her only resulted in missing them more.

Next time, she would concentrate on her other purpose: to find a friend to chat with. But not on any of the multiple websites advertised as the most successful dating sites. They were too invasive and the pictures uncomfortably inappropriate. Besides, dating could never happen for her, and she didn't want to put anything personal out there in case Uncle Filip somehow found out. Yes, she would focus on looking for someone to chat with, like Franklin. Beloved, old Franklin.

17

OMANI

It was late. Omani sat in the kitchen alone wrapping cutlery into white linen napkins monogrammed with a red V. December was always so dreary now. As a child, she and her mother would decorate with wreaths and colorful ornaments, and even a sprig of mistletoe. The house smelled of baking sugar cookies and fudge. Omani hadn't felt like putting up a tree once her mother had passed. Uncle Filip did not celebrate anything, and every day was just like any other day of the year.

Meals for the next couple of days would be simplified and take longer to make with a skeleton crew, yet it was worth allowing more of her employees to be with their families over the holidays. She didn't want to be like Filip who refused to give any of his employees time away. He didn't interfere with the way she managed her workers as long as things were taken care of. She wondered how she could spend so much of her life interacting with other people and still feel so lonely.

After finishing her last set-up, she stood in front of an industrial-sized refrigerator door perusing the selection of meats inside. She touched the labels thinking about how her Uncle always insisted on the highest grade of everything with nothing unnatural or genetically modified. That was one of few areas in which Omani and he agreed. This meant higher food costs, but

Mr. Bisch had his sources and always came through with Omani's requests despite his grumbling about the extra effort it took.

Once in a while she liked cooking for herself to enjoy some peaceful solitude without interruptions from needy employees. She would not rush. Anyway, she had nowhere to go. Omani selected a veal chop. She turned on some soft piano music, poured a glass of pinot noir, and began her preparations.

Two glasses of vino and an hour later, she sat down to her meal—tender sliced veal with sweetbreads sautéed in a gravy of onions, butter, white wine, cream, and mushrooms, and hot French bread with basil infused olive oil dipping sauce. She recalled the night her mother had taught her to prepare that exact meal. Omani was sixteen years old.

"You need to learn how to cook," her mother told her. "Someday you'll want to do this for your own family."

"I'm gonna marry a guy who knows how to do all that stuff."

Hanna raised a brow and handed her several mushrooms. "That'd be nice. In the meantime, wash these."

Omani complied. Her stomach rumbled. All the smells wafted through the air while Hanna combined the spices and ingredients. The meal was delicious, as usual.

Mother and daughter's conversation revolved around school, work, and planning their next getaway to the Amalfi Coast. As Omani reluctantly did her least favorite chore at the end of dinner, the dishes, her mom returned to her office.

Omani heard a gasp and called out, "Mom?" With no reply, she dried her hands, grabbed her crutches, and walked to the office door. Hanna sat with a hand clasped over her mouth, staring at her monitor. "Mom? What's up?"

Tears brimmed in her mother's eyes.

Omani's heart sped up. "What happened? Did somebody die?"

Hanna rose and gave her daughter a tight hug. "It worked."

She felt her mother trembling. "What worked?"

"I got a response."

"You mean?" Omani pointed to the computer, her eyes wide. "From who? An alien?"

Grabbing the sides of her head, Hanna paced. "It doesn't matter."

Omani went to the screen to see a single word displayed.

Hello?

"Mom!"

Her mother dropped into her office chair and stared at the salutation.

"It only took like seven years," said Omani, excitedly. "What are you gonna say?" Hanna tapped her fingers against her chin. "Aren't you going to answer?"

Her mother shook her head. "Julia needs to be here."

"No. Really? Come on."

Hanna powered down her computer. "It can wait."

"Seriously, Mom? You could at least find out what planet it's from?"

"I'm tired," said Hanna.

"Well, I'm not."

Hanna switched the desk light off. "You've got school tomorrow and I have to work. I'll respond later."

Omani rolled her eyes. "Geez, that's so dumb."

"You cannot tell any of your friends. Don't mention this to anyone, alright?"

"I don't even know what *this* is," protested Omani. "Why not?"

"Just don't. Finish cleaning up and go to bed."

Omani gave an over-dramatic, teenager sigh. "I don't get you sometimes."

Hanna embraced her daughter. "Good night, honey. I love you."

"Love you too." Omani watched her mother go to her bedroom. How could she be so calm?

Omani chuckled at how frustrated she'd been with her mother that night. She dipped her last piece of bread in the oil, and swallowed her final sip of wine. She badly wanted to return to her room and type her own *hello*, but it was late and also the holidays for many in the world. People would be traveling and busy with family. Omani didn't want to admit to herself that she was actually rather nervous to reach out. Maybe it wouldn't work. Maybe no one would be interested in being friends with her. She should wait a few more days.

18

TREAZ

Treaz returned to Bella's work. She kept the secret of the cancer diagnosis to herself. Early in her shift, Beckman arrived to the coffee shop by himself, carrying his notepad.

"Where's your mom today?" she asked.

"She's sick."

Treaz tried not to show her satisfaction for his mother being absent. "Anything serious?"

He shook his head. "Just a cold. She took some medicine that made her sleepy." He glanced over his shoulder. "She would freak if she knew I was here."

Treaz wanted to take advantage of the opportunity to have a conversation with him. His continued drawings and notes intrigued her. "I'm going on my lunch break soon. You want some company?"

Beckman stammered. "Uh, sure."

"Great. Let's sit outside."

He looked down at the floor. "I don't fit in the chairs."

Treaz internally kicked herself. It must be awkward for him being so large. "There's a low wall along the south side of the patio. Would that work? I don't want to be under my boss's nose." Beckman nodded. "I'm off the clock in ten. I'll catch up with you." Treaz headed to check on the status of the restrooms. She noticed that Beckman ordered a large coffee, no food, and went outside to wait.

When she approached him sitting on the wall, he looked quite substantial on the brick. Guilt flared as she realized it wasn't as comfortable as being inside, but it was more private. She brought them each a macaroon, and he accepted it politely.

"So Beckman, can I ask you about your mom? She seems a bit over zealous."

He sighed. "She's got good intentions."

Treaz maintained a positive expression despite being unsure about a mother force-feeding her already obese son.

"It's hard to meet anyone. I'm not exactly the most desirable guy on the patio," he said with a smirk.

"I think there's a good guy in there."

"I'm the size of three guys."

"More to like." Treaz smiled, but observed the smallest clench in his jaw. *He doesn't like himself.* "Beckman, does one of those guys want to escape?"

He nodded. "All three."

Treaz instantly regretted bringing the macaroons. Hers was half gone, his untouched. She pointed at the fattening sugar mass. "Sorry about that."

Beckman waved his hand. "People assume I want to eat myself into oblivion, and honestly, most of the time I do."

"But, not all the time?"

"No."

She had to change topics. "Do you work?"

"Not a real job. I mess around with programming."

"I bet you're good at it."

Beckman frowned. "Why would you think that? All you've seen is me shoving food in my face."

Sheepishly, she took the discarded pages from her pocket and handed them to him. "I don't understand what this is all about, but it looks really important."

Beckman grinned a little. "Are you spying on me?"

Treaz shook her head. "No. I mean I didn't mean it that way. I just was curious why you always throw everything away?"

"Because my mom thinks I'm a complete failure and doesn't believe I can program anything significant." Beckman rubbed the back of his head. "I think she's afraid I'll move away, and she'll be alone." He paused in thought. "I do love her. She's always taken care of me."

"At some point you have to live your own life and make your own decisions." Maybe Beckman was her Asset. She turned to face him on the wall. "When I went away to college, it felt so wonderful to be on my own. My grandmother still loved me even though she was heartbroken to see me go. I'd lived with her since I was nine."

"My mom acted the same way when I left for college," he said. "I screwed things up the first time, so I don't think I'll convince her to let me try again."

Despite her fear of sounding preachy, she continued. "It's not a matter of convincing her. Most parents want their child to be successful. Whether you go back to school or go to work, this is your life to live. Not your mother's."

He stroked his scruffy beard.

"I became a responsible adult, and was making my own choices. My grandmother was so proud at my graduation." Suddenly, she remembered where she had seen Pearl Man before —at her graduation ten years ago. She sipped her coffee to hide her surprise memory.

As Treaz filed into the stadium with all the other graduates with their caps and gowns, she caught a man looking at her. She didn't think anything of it as he quickly blended in the crowd of well-wishers cheering on their loved ones. But she had noticed his white earring. Treaz knew she'd seen Pearl Man before, and she'd confront him next time he came to see her. Why would he lie about not being around her?

Treaz spent the rest of her lunch period persuading Beckman to step out on his own. When she got up to leave, he reached out to shake her hand. "Thanks for talking to me, Treaz. And for seeing me as a real human."

Her heart warmed. "You're welcome. Something tells me that you've got amazing things to do."

"Your manager won't be so happy," he added. Treaz cocked her head. "Your dessert sales are going to drop significantly."

A pain shot through her neck, and she massaged it. "I hope your mother feels better."

On the way home from work Treaz kept expecting to "disappear". When that didn't happen she surmised maybe this whole experience was a kind of reincarnation. Perhaps she needed to learn something to move on to the next stage, or she was being trained for something bigger and more significant. If this was the case, she hoped to soon master everything and be finished with it all.

Later that night, Treaz answered a knock at Bella's door. It was Pearl Man. "How's your assignment progressing?"

"You don't know?" Treaz mocked.

"I want to hear what you think about it," he answered walking into the apartment without invitation.

She shared her breakthrough with Beckman and insisted he should be her Asset even if Pearl Man didn't agree. Also she mentioned thinking she'd found another Transitioner.

"She thought I was nuts—which I'm still not convinced that I'm not."

"Others are out there, but you can't speculate someone's a Transitioner."

Her mouth opened, it was true. "Can you introduce me to some?"

"No."

Treaz grimaced. "How about just one? It would be like on-the-job training."

"It's against policy."

She put her hands on her hips. "Whose policy?"

Pearl Man ignored the question.

Treaz slipped in a chair to sulk. "I wish I wouldn't have lost my job because then I probably wouldn't be here."

He tilted his head. "Do you know what happened?"

"My supervisor called me in and said they didn't need my services any longer. Crappy after working for them for over three years."

"Those are tricky situations."

"Not really. They didn't like something I did, let me go, and didn't have the decency to tell me what it was. Made me feel terrible."

He hesitated before responding. "You didn't do anything wrong." She glared at him. Pearl Man reached up and twisted his earring. "On occasion, things like that happen when a Transitioner is needed."

Was she getting his drift? "What'd you do, call up my boss and tell him I was taking a new job?"

"Pretty much."

Treaz jumped to her feet. "Wow. It would have been nice to be asked if I even *wanted* this ludicrous job."

He nodded. "I understand."

"No, you don't. Otherwise, I wouldn't be here. How'd I get picked to do this dumb job anyway?"

Pearl Man released air through pursed lips, staring at the table. "Having few connections with other people is a big plus. Individuals who keep to themselves more."

"Loners."

He folded his hands. "Typically introverts are better to bring on board because there's less disruption. An adult child with no parents or children. One without a partner or family ties. With fewer people in their lives, it's easier."

"None of this is easy," she argued. "And what about my grandmother? I'm very close to her."

"Though she isn't in the best frame of mind," he said.

"What do you care?" she spat out at him. Treaz thought about Grammie, her worsening dementia, and her inability to remember if Treaz visited every day, month, or even year. She was simply happy when her granddaughter came. Pearl Man's description characterized Treaz to a tee. She didn't have friends, was unemployed, and aside from Grammie, had no other family. She was a loner. "There's tons of depressed, introverted, lonely people. What makes me so unique?"

"You are special, Treaz. You're softer spoken, compassionate, can get closer to people. You don't come across as intimidating."

She exhaled a long breath. "I guess I should be flattered. But, I'm not always all those things."

"You've a rare skill of influencing in a way that works better with certain Assets."

"I'm still confused about why you use Transitioners at all. Can't you just make the Assets do what you want?"

"There's more power in someone wanting to do something on their own as opposed to being forced," Pearl Man explained. "Being pushed into an action or decision they aren't ready for can mean burn out, quitting. Sometimes it leads to substance abuse or suicide."

When Treaz worked past jobs she hated, life became miserable and unfulfilling. Kind of the way she was feeling as a Transitioner—although, she had to admit, only to herself, that it *had* felt satisfying to think she may have helped Beckman.

"For any number of reasons people get stuck, allowing distractions to stop them from reaching their full potential," he said. "That's why Transitioners are so vital. They persuade Assets to believe they have the capability of doing something. Not necessarily only one thing, but often a first step gives them the confidence to move forward, and in turn build competence. You might think of yourself as a type of career advisor or guidance counselor. Because of you, people are able to do things that they never thought they could."

Could her position be more altruistic than she formerly imagined? She certainly never thought of herself as being in a helping profession. Her charitable musings were short lived. "So, us Transitioners manipulate people to chase down their passions and dreams, while we're enslaved doing some corporation's bidding."

He got up from his chair.

"I knew I saw you before. It was at my college graduation. I remember your earring." She watched him glance away. "That was ten years ago. Why were you there?"

After a long pause, it came out. "Yes, I was there."

She clapped her hands. "I knew it."

137

"I was attempting to stop Vanguard from taking you, yet."

"Wasn't that thoughtful of you. Is that the name of our employer, Vanguard?" He nodded. "I'm going to look them up and find out what the hell they're all about."

"You can't find them online," Pearl Man said. He walked to the door. "Time to go."

"I still have questions."

"I know."

She motioned at herself. "Did you know that the woman who's body I'm currently in has cancer?"

He stopped. "I did not."

"Well, you should tell your recruiters to do a better background check. Bella needs proper healthcare. Does Vanguard offer benefits? Do they have an insurance plan?"

"You still have sleeping pills?" he asked. She nodded. "Take two, Treaz. You could use some rest."

As she waited for sleep, she wondered why Pearl Man had held off Vanguard from recruiting her earlier. Before coming to any sensible conclusions, she fell into a deep slumber.

19

OMANI

Early on December 26, Omani buzzed around peeling potatoes, frying bacon and eggs, and melting raclette cheese for the preparation of rosti. She'd been pulling double duty in the kitchen and housekeeping areas since many of her staff were celebrating winter holidays. The late nights and early mornings kept her from spending any more time on the internet.

As she anticipated her upcoming foray into finding a friend online, she thought back to her mother. Hanna and Julia had responded to the first return message of the 'Hello' before Omani had returned from school so she didn't know what had been said.

When Omani arrived home, Hanna turned off the computer and took her to Shelby's for dinner. She was cryptic in her description of the conversation with the stranger at the other end of the computer.

"So is it an alien that lives on some weird planet or something?" asked Omani.

Hanna laughed. "He is an alien but only because he lives in the United States."

Slightly disappointed that he wasn't a little green man from Mars, Omani remained intrigued. "America? Really? Is he super rich?"

"Oh Ani. Not every American is a millionaire," said Hanna.

"What's he do?"

"He works on computers."

Omani's shoulders dropped. "That's all? Why'd it take seven years to write back if he's so smart?"

Her mother shrugged.

Another week passed and Omani cornered her mother for the twentieth time. "Mom, can I message the guy in America?"

Hanna shook her head. "I don't know."

"You've been talking for forever now. You gotta have an idea if he's a serial killer or something." Her mother laughed. "What's the big deal?" Omani pressed. "Why do only you and Julia get to talk with him?"

Her mother bit her lip. "I'll have to ask." Two days later, Hanna delivered the news. "Franklin said he would chat with you."

"Finally!" exclaimed Omani starting for the office.

"After homework and supper," clarified Hanna to her daughter's rolling eyes. "He'll be sleeping anyway. There's a nine hour time difference."

Omani looked at the time, then rushed to do her school work. She gobbled down her zucchini spaghetti and chicken meatball dinner, finished the dishes, and got all ready for bed.

She sat in front of the computer trying to decide what to say first. "Should I call him Franklin or Mr. Franklin?"

"Franklin would probably be fine."

Omani turned around and gave her mother a look when she didn't leave. "You don't have to watch me."

Hanna put up her hands, turned, and walked to the door. "Bed in fifteen."

"Mom!" But the standard consequences of breaking her mother's rules meant being grounded for a week with no internet or video games. "Alright." She rubbed her palms together, then typed her first contact.

OL: Hi Franklin. I'm Hanna's daughter, Omani.

She waited for his reply which came quickly.

FM: Hello Omani. Nice to meet you. How are you?

"He sounds normal," she muttered.

OL: I'm fine. How are you?
FM: Doing well, thank you. Your mother tells me that you're sixteen.
OL: Yeah. How old are you? Oh, is it cool that I call you Franklin?
FM: Sure. I just turned thirty-two.

He was three years younger than her mom. Might her mother be interested in Franklin in a romantic way? They certainly had been doing a lot of messaging. Of course, Switzerland and the USA were really far apart, but you never know what might happen. She must do a little investigating.

OL: Are you married?
FM: I am. And we've got a kid on the way.

"So much for that," lamented Omani aloud.

OL: Congratulations.

FM: Thanks. I understand you lost your dad when you were young.

OL: Yeah. Mom keeps a couple pictures of the three of us around, but I don't have any memories of him.

FM: I'm sorry, Omani.

OL: It's fine. I guess I can't be too depressed about someone I never knew. The worst part is my Uncle Filip is always trying to act like he's my father. He's just seriously a pain.

She looked at the time again, but before Omani could type anything else, Franklin sent his next message.

FM: Well, your mom allowed fifteen minutes, so time's about up.

OL: Ugh! Did my mother recruit you to be like a dad?

FM: That's very funny. No. I've got to go. I hope we can chat again some time.

Omani did have lots of questions to ask him. Where exactly did he live? When was his baby due? What did he do for fun in America?

OL: Yes. That'd be cool.

FM: Good night.

OL: Good day.

Remembering back to her first conversation with Franklin made Omani enthusiastic to send her own message—find her own present day Franklin. Was she too old to get so excited? Who cared?

Since her Uncle's company was recognized by the nation as waging war against terrorism, and he gave his employees one week off for each three weeks worked, Swiss labor laws were not enforceable on the Compound. Omani sometimes heard people complaining about not being granted the full winter holiday which normally extended until January 1st. Yet everyone needed their jobs so they followed Vanguard's rules and returned to work on December 27th.

Omani stood in the kitchen calculating in her head the amount of ingredients needed to make thirteen kiwi pies. Fritter had insisted on preparing a special dessert for New Year's Day.

"People will go for seconds," said Omani to an employee making notes of what to order. "So, include extra on the normal items, like eggs and sugar. Then add nine boxes of graham crackers, three kilograms of macadamias, and seven dozen kiwis."

"You're smart, doing all that in your head," said the worker.

"I paid attention in math class," Omani said as she took her crutches and left. She recalled Franklin's and her conversation about that very subject.

For several weeks before bed, Omani had enjoyed her regular sessions with Franklin. They covered many topics, and she never ran out of questions to ask. He openly answered most of them while evading others, which she figured meant she was getting too personal. He asked a lot about her life as well, and genuinely seemed interested.

One night Franklin inquired about how her day at school had gone.

OL: Terrible.
FM: What happened?
OL: I blew my math test.
FM: You usually do well on your exams.

Omani leaned back in her chair wondering if Franklin told her mother every word of their conversations. She hoped not. She didn't want to admit that all her grades were beginning to edge downward.

FM: Why was this one different?
OL: I guess, I didn't study enough. School's so boring.
FM: Ah, yes. I remember feeling that way as well.
OL: They make us memorize tons of dates and events that I could easily look up online. And when am I ever going to use an algebraic formula? It's just busy work.

Omani turned, making sure her mother had not entered the room. She would pitch a fit if she found out Omani wasn't trying at school.

FM: I know it seems that way now. In fact honestly, some of it is pretty useless. But you'll be surprised how much of the information will come in handy.
OL: Whatever.
FM: Really. If you're serious about being a doctor like your mother, that requires studying to keep those school marks up. College will be even tougher.

As much as she liked Franklin, he was also an adult. How could she expect him to say anything different?

OL: It's more entertaining to have discussions about important things with my friends, and you.

FM: Sometimes to be successful, we have to do more things we don't like, and less things we enjoy.

OL: You sound like my mom.

FM: She's an intelligent woman. You should listen to her.

The adults must have conspired.

FM: I'd better sign off. Don't want your mom mad at me for keeping you from your studies.

The next evening Omani and Franklin had their customary fifteen minute chat.

FM: I got a confession to make.

She sat forward. Not many adults wanted to confess to a teenager—like any of them.

FM: I might not be able to communicate as much with you and your mom.

Omani didn't ask her mother what she and Franklin discussed. It was probably only dull thirty-year-olds kind of stuff anyway. Yet, Omani didn't want to stop messaging.

OL: No, wait. I promise I'll study for my tests.

FM: You'd better! But I've been unemployed for a while now and my wife's been all over me to find a job.

OL: You've been looking, right?

FM: Of course. I'm just not receiving any offers. Money's getting tight.

OL: There has to be something me or my mom can do. If you lived closer, you could work at her office as a computer guy.

FM: You're very thoughtful, Omani. There isn't anything either of you can do, although I appreciate the offer.

Omani went to bed with her mind full. Franklin kind of acted like a father. Not the disciplining type, like her overbearing Uncle Filip, but like a cool one. The next morning she talked to her mother about the situation.

"We gotta help him," Omani pleaded. "He sounded really down."

"I'll see what I can do," Hanna said.

Omani never found out what her mother had done to help Franklin, but he seemed to overcome his financial problems quickly. To thank them, he sent her mother some money to give to Omani.

"He said for you to buy something nice for yourself," her mother told her.

Omani recalled she had purchased books and music with the money from Franklin. Yet the best part was that he continued messaging with both Omani and her mother until…well, until everything changed.

20
TREAZ

Treaz awoke to an offensive odor of old sweat and urine. She rubbed her nose and realized the smell came from the blanket covering her naked body. Throwing it off, she sat up. Her feet hit the floor hard as there was no box spring, just a lumpy mattress. She had Advanced again. How could anyone ever get used to such an abrupt process?

It was dark, yet there was a hint of light peeking from behind whatever covered the window. A scuffling sound came from a few feet away. "Is somebody there?" Something furry brushed against her foot, and she jumped to the center of the bed, hugging her knees close, her heart pounding. *Oh God.* Could that be a—she refused to utter or think the word. She didn't want to name the vermin. Her uninvited guest scuttled from one side of the room to the other. Treaz searched for a bedside lamp. The one she found had no bulb. Another scurry.

Treaz clapped her hands several times, cringing as she placed her bare feet back in the danger zone. "I'm getting up. I'm moving," she yelled. "Get out of my way. Get out." She walked with outstretched arms. "Go away. Go away."

She reached a wall and found a switch hoping the animal had escaped so she wouldn't have to see it. When the overhead lightbulb illuminated the small room, the five-inch black rat bolted along the mattress and into a corner. Treaz shifted rapidly from foot to foot, her breathing heavy. "Oh God. Oh God."

The ugly creature stared back at her with one beady black eye —the other a scarred-over pit. "Go away," she shouted and swung her arms wildly praying it was more frightened than she. The rat dashed through a crack in the wall. In a flash, Treaz grabbed a crumpled dress from the floor and shoved it in the gap, trusting that would keep the little horror from reemerging anytime soon. Whoever's apartment she was in needed serious pest control.

The cramped studio was barely furnished. A garbage bag hung with duct tape over the window. It bulged with the breeze. Piles of clothes were entangled with discarded trash.

"This is horrible." Treaz cradled the sides of her throbbing head, the aching was worse than the other two times she woke in another's body.

Her bladder screamed for relief. As she walked to the bathroom, which had no door on its hinges, the grittiness from the floor—a mixture of dirt and food particles, adhered to her soles. No wonder the rodent was there.

The scum in the toilet bowl and mold in the shower made her gag. Spiders had taken up residency across the light fixture. She shut her eyes and squatted over the commode refusing to touch anything. Her thigh muscles stung as she held position and counted for almost ninety seconds—anything to distract from her latest nightmare.

The cracked mirror reflected back a short, scrawny woman. Dark circles below and over-grown eyebrows above accented hollow eyes. At least her complexion was clear. A bonus— literally, the *only* positive.

She found ripped jeans and a stained blouse on the floor, swallowed her disgust, and slipped them on. A worn pair of flip flops would protect her feet from the filth.

Treaz needed a stiff drink to take the edge off her growing anxiety. It didn't matter that the stove clock read 9:17 am. In the almost empty kitchen cabinets, she found three cans of soup and a box of saltine crackers. Next to it, a bottle of Bankers Club Bourbon with a couple shots worth gracing the bottom. Immediately she hoisted it to her lips and emptied the contents. It burned going down. The liquor gave her an almost instant buzz, and she fell into one of two mismatched kitchen chairs to open the familiar box set on the table.

Inside was an expired driver's license for Zoe Landis, age thirty-one. There was no credit card, no phone, just a bus pass, a route map, a twenty dollar bill, a food stamp debit card, the standard pouch of sleeping pills, and an appointment reminder for a meeting with a job counselor. The post-it note attached stated: *Today. Bus Route 13.*

"Gee. Thanks for the tip, Pearl Man," she said sarcastically.

Shouting erupted from the apartment next door. Through the paper thin walls, she heard every word audible between two women screaming expletive-laden accusations at each other.

She wanted to flee from this hell hole. Where was Pearl Man? How could Vanguard expect their Transitioners to work in such squalid and disgusting conditions? What a scam of an organization, trapping their employees, knowing that if they talk, people will assume they're crazy. *Is this how they encourage employee retention?* She would refuse to do it any longer. Surely, Pearl Man would show up soon. He wouldn't leave her in this type of assignment alone. She numbly picked at the scab on her upper, inner arm.

Maybe the alcohol without food wasn't such a grand idea. She didn't want to end up in another psych ward trying to explain someone else's life. She loathed the thought of cooking in Zoe's kitchen, but she must eat something. A line of ants trailed from the sink drain to the inside of a greasy toaster oven. More insects gathered at sticky jelly drops left on the chipped tile. In the cupboard, a large cockroach sat in the corner. Grabbing the nearest can and the cracker box, she quickly slammed the door. Finding only an empty container of dish soap, she ran scalding water in a pot for five minutes. Yanking on a jammed drawer, she located a can opener stuck to an ice-cream scoop. She heated the tomato soup until it was steamy, and consumed it directly from the pan. The crackers were stale, but she ate them anyway.

Two hours later, Treaz figured Pearl Man had abandoned her, so she took the items from the box and left the apartment. The neglected building circled a central garden area overrun with weeds and dog feces. Two dodgy-looking neighbors stood talking, but she ignored their stares and passed by, her head down. As she walked down the street, the chilly air made Treaz wish she had brought a jacket. Her clothes smelled rancid, skin itched, and hair demanded shampoo. *This Zoe chick's a mess.* Could a Host body also be an Asset? If so, she'd concentrate on cleaning Zoe up.

A bus stop was close by, and her transportation arrived in a flurry of exhaust. She climbed on, running her pass through the machine. Before exiting, she asked the driver about the address. He motioned her down the road two blocks. Inside the red stucco building, Treaz found the correct suite. Seven people sat quietly waiting. The receptionist texted non-stop on her phone.

Treaz tapped on the glass. "Excuse me. I have an appointment."

Without looking up, the woman opened the window. "Name?"

"Zoe Landis."

"You're late," the receptionist said.

"It took longer than—"

"You were just here." The woman arched a brow. "Why are you back so soon?"

"I'm here because of this." Treaz held up the Post-It note. "Is there a problem?" The sliding window banged closed in Treaz's face. She sat next to a man wearing a button-down shirt with a rip in the sleeve.

"We call her, Miss Cheery," he said. "Don't take it personal."

"I don't know why she doesn't get fired."

He shrugged. "Management doesn't care. She was probably siting in one of these chairs not long ago."

"Still. Are you here to find a job?" Treaz asked.

He gave a tight-lipped smile. "Rumor has it."

"What kind do they offer?"

"It's usually pretty basic. Housecleaning, construction cleanup, sign twirling."

"Sign twirling?"

He scooped up a magazine, attempting to spin it on his middle finger. "You know those people on street corners tossing around a cardboard sign to entice people into a store, or to get their taxes done?" The magazine fell, sprawled out on the floor. Miss Cheery looked up and scowled.

"I didn't make it a day in that job."

Treaz chuckled. Could this guy be her Asset?

Miss Cheery slid open the glass window, and pointed at him.

"So cheery," Treaz joked.

"Yup. One of a kind." He disappeared through a door, and reappeared ten minutes later. "Dishwasher at a Mexican dive. Can't wait to scrape dried refried beans off ceramic plates." He waved as he left. "Good luck. See you in a week."

Treaz hoped not, because if he was her Asset, that meant she'd be stuck being Zoe Landis for too long. The window opened six more times before Miss Cheery pointed and frowned at Treaz.

She entered an under-sized office. A woman stood with her short arms buried in a cabinet drawer. The name plate read Mrs. Williams, and Treaz sat down. The woman turned, dropping a thick folder on the desk.

"Zoe, what happened at the dry cleaners?"

"I don't know." She honestly did not.

"Those jobs don't come often. It was an excellent opportunity for you." Mrs. Williams shook her head, and opened the over-stuffed file indicating to Treaz that Zoe had trouble holding down a job. "You've been through a lot of positions. Every time you're absent and don't bother to call, clients stop listing with us."

"I can do better," Treaz said. She was responsible and knew how to show up for work, unlike Zoe. "I just need another chance."

"You're running out of those."

"Please, I promise."

"Heard it before," said Mrs. Williams. "I might have something in a couple weeks."

Treaz leaned forward. "What am I supposed to do in the meantime?"

The woman handed Treaz an appointment reminder. "Best I can do."

"But," Treaz tried to protest. "What am I going to—"

Mrs. Williams waved Treaz away and removed the next client folder.

That was bad news. Here she was probably living in a crack-house, with hardly any food or money, and couldn't get a job. She wanted to lodge a complaint with Pearl Man—like that would work.

On the way back to the bus stop, she saw a local bar with graffiti on the door and bars on the windows. With the twenty in her pocket she could afford a drink or two to figure things out.

21

TREAZ

It took a few moments for Treaz's eyes to adjust to the dimness of the bar. A man by himself strummed an imaginary guitar. Two men at a back table consoled each other with clumsy movements and droopy eyelids. She gave a sideways smile. *Drunk people helping drunk people*. If she only had someone to talk to. That idiot Pearl Man.

She sat on a barstool unsure she wanted to put any part of her body near the marred counter decorated with ketchup stains, peanut shells, and condensation rings. But, in Zoe's body, what did it matter?

Behind the counter was a tattoo-covered bulging muscled man who appeared more like a bouncer than a bartender. He served a burger and fries to a woman, then came to Treaz. "Hello, Zoe. The usual?"

He knew her—or rather Zoe. "Remind me of your name?" she asked.

He furrowed his brow. "Really?"

So awkward. "Sorry. Just forgetful today."

"Garry."

"Right. Sure, I'll take the usual." She might as well find out her Host's choice of poison.

He stood waiting, and Treaz cocked her head at him. "Rules haven't changed, Zoe. You gotta pay in advance."

Treaz hadn't been to an excessive number of bars in her life, but none of them required paying before you got your order. She pulled out the twenty dollars and slid it across the bar. He snatched it up, and returned with the change. She dropped the coins in the tip jar. Garry raised his eyebrows, then nodded an acknowledgement.

How often had Zoe frequented this place? Probably every time she came to see the amiable Mrs. Williams. She figured the woman was trying to help, but apparently Zoe had not been a good girl. Why couldn't she hold down a job?

Garry delivered the drink. A screwdriver! How fitting—the same poisonous choice Treaz had downed the night of her birthday. She quickly drank half of it on the first go. It was perfect—light on the orange juice and heavy on the vodka. In no time she paid for and finished her second one at which point a slight dizziness kicked in and she settled back in her seat.

"You want some water?" Garry asked.

"How long have you known me?"

He inhaled. "Two, three years?"

She nodded. "What kind of person am I?"

Before he could answer, a familiar voice came from behind her.

"Give her a water. I'll take a Coke."

"Oh, now you show," Treaz said sarcastically. She picked up her empty glass and called out to Garry. "I'll take another one. This guy's buying." Pearl Man nodded at the bartender. She lifted her hands towards Garry. "How come he doesn't have to pay in advance?"

Pearl Man sat next to her.

"I'm going to the police," she said.

He shook his head. "I wouldn't advise that. Remember what happened last time you told someone?"

"Yeah. I ended up in the loony bin." Treaz twisted her chair to face him. "I got a request for you, oh boss of mine."

"Technically, my title is a Counselor."

She grimaced. Another counselor, just what she needed. "Alright then, oh Counselor of mine, I want a friend." He shook his head. "Why not? You expect me to go through all this and not be able to talk to anyone?"

He touched his chest. "You can talk to me."

"You?" She laughed. "No, I mean another Transitioner. Someone who can really understand everything we have to go through."

"I told you before, not possible."

"Oh yeah. 'Cuz it's against Vanguard policy," she mocked. "Don't you ever break the rules, Pearl Man?"

Garry brought their drinks.

She held hers up and spoke to it. "Guess it's just you and me, then." She chugged several gulps as Pearl Man sipped his soda. "You can't just yank people out of their existing lives to do your bidding," she said. "Would you and your horrible Vanguard organization have pulled me out of my life for forced labor if I was still involved with Tim? Would you still have brought me into your nasty little world?"

He shifted in his seat. "I didn't bring—"

"Admit it, Mr. P. You're responsible. Tell me. If me and my boyfriend hadn't have broken up, would I be here?"

"You had a boyfriend?"

She scoffed. "You had to know!" He shook his head. "Well, let me tell you about my Tim. He was a decent guy. We had this pretty serious thing going for awhile."

"How'd you meet him?"

She smiled recalling the restaurant she'd taken her grandmother to a few years before. The café had been one of Treaz's favorites.

Treaz set their customer number on the table and she and her grandmother waited. Grammie talked about the cozy decor and the chef's tall hats. The whole place smelled of baking bread and cinnamon.

After ten minutes, a man around thirty set down their meal. "Here you go, ladies."

"Thank you," said Grammie. "My granddaughter raves about your French onion soup."

Treaz hadn't expected to be silenced by his shining blue eyes and flop of blonde hair. Her heart sped when he flashed a stunning smile.

"Made daily from Vidalia onions, topped with our homemade baguettes, and smothered in both Gruyère and parmesan," he said.

"Mmm, sounds delicious." Grammie squinted at his name tag. "What a pleasant young man you are, Tim. Quite handsome as well. Are you single?"

"Grammie," Treaz whispered, certain her burning face glowed all shades of red.

Tim placed his hand over his heart. "You are quite a beauty, Grammie. Are you asking me on a date?"

Her grandmother roared with laughter. "Oh heavens no. But, Treaz is single—"

Mortified, Treaz dropped her gaze to the steaming soup wishing she could crawl into the bowl. "Grammie, please."

Tim chuckled, then tilted his head toward Treaz. "I like your name."

She concentrated on keeping her breathing steady. Under the table, she gripped her thighs with sweaty palms. "Thank you," she managed to say. Why did she get so tongue-tied around hot guys?

Tim raised his index finger. "Be right back."

Treaz leaned close to her grandmother. "Please stop trying to find a man for me."

"Someone has to do it," said Grammie stirring in the melted cheese and taking a taste. "Lordy, this is as good as mine. The cook at the nursing home needs lessons."

Tim reappeared with two warm, golden croissants. "On the house."

Treaz's mouth watered, then she looked at the pastries.

"These things will melt in your mouth," he offered refusing to unlock his eyes from hers when she glanced up again.

Pearl Man interrupted her thoughts. "Were you going to marry him?"

Treaz blinked back unexpected tears. Tim wasn't perfect, but neither was she. He had loved her grandmother though, which meant so much to her. She took another long sip. "Maybe. We dated for almost four years. Then he cheated on me with his ex, even though he swore he didn't. I saw a picture of them. I was so angry. I told him we were done."

"That's rough," Pearl Man commented.

"It happens," she said. "A couple weeks later his sister called me. He was on his way to my house to convince me to take him back when he got killed in a car accident."

Pearl Man sipped his Coke.

"Yo, Greg?" shouted Treaz.

"The name's Garry."

"Whatever. You got any banker bourbon?"

"What?"

"Bankrupt bourbon. I need a shot."

"You don't need any more," said Pearl Man.

Garry shrugged. "Never heard of it."

She pointed at Pearl Man. "Well get me another of those yellow screwup drinks and put it on his bill."

Pearl Man tried to protest. "I don't think—"

She slurred her words. "You're my employer, and since you decided to make me dirt poor and can't afford to buy my own, you owe it to me. Besides, I'm sure you've got some extravagant expense account."

"Treaz. You need to be careful with the drinking."

She slapped her hand on the counter making the other patrons look over. "Who cares? This is perfectly justified. I've already spent the night in restraints, had to clean filthy toilets, and now I live in an absolute hell hole with rats and cockroaches and can't even get a shitty job." Treaz arched her brows at her own language, then laughed. "Go Zoe."

"Unfortunately, sometimes that's the work," Pearl Man said.

"What ever happened with Beckman? Did I get fired from that assignment too, like my old job?"

"No, you were successful," he said.

Her eyebrows raised. "And I get thanked by ending up here, like this? Some way to reward your employees. Why can't I just be in a *normal* person's body?"

He tilted his head. "*Normal?*"

"Yeah, you know, someone without an addiction, or can hold a job, or isn't having to deal with acne or cancer or whatever. Will every Host I live in have problems?"

Her Counselor pushed his soda to the side. "Were you *normal*, Treaz? Was your life worry-free? Did you have everything you ever needed or wanted? I'd like to know your definition of *normal.*"

160

She chewed on her lower lip.

He continued. "I can't imagine everything in your life was perfect or *normal*, as you put it. You're going to find yourself in some less than desirable circumstances and in the Hosts of people vastly different from yourself—older, younger, varying ethnicities. You are going to get a good dose of reality in this work. When you're done, we can talk about *normal*."

She grabbed his arm, her voice dripped with sarcasm. "Hey, you know what's hilarious? I never signed up for this job. At first, I thought perhaps you were some kind of angel. But, I was wrong. I think you're more of an evil demon."

He stood.

She could tell she hurt his feelings, but didn't stop chiding. "Do you enjoy your job? Like putting people through all this?"

Pearl Man waved Garry over and handed him cash. "No more for her." He turned to Treaz speaking quiet and stern. "Don't make things worse for you or Zoe."

"Is that s'pposed to make me feel guilty? You don't care." He walked away. She called out after him. "See, I'm not such a nice person after all. Just look at my compassion now. You need to fire me." No response. "Come on, P. Fire my ass." As he exited the door, she yelled out a final sentiment. "I miss my Grammie. She's gonna be so pissed when she figures out I've been kidnapped."

"Zoe," said Garry. "Go home."

Treaz gave him a scowl, got up, and left. She did her best to keep her head up and walk without staggering. Treaz knew she was failing miserably.

She stumbled down the sidewalk from the bar and into a small convenience store. Zoe definitely needed more than soup. The clerk eyed her warily as she wandered the aisles. Her mouth watered at the glistening hot dogs rolling under the heating lamp. Treaz took one, slipped it in a bun, and smothered it with mustard and relish. She served herself a cup of coffee, picked up a bag of off-brand potato chips, a prepared turkey sandwich wrapped in plastic, and approached the front trying to juggle everything. It all scattered onto the counter.

The cashier rang up the total. "$11.02," he said cooly. Treaz pulled out Zoe's food stamp card.

"Oh." He held up the chips. "This is the only thing you can buy with the card."

She frowned. "What?"

The clerk swept his hand over the other items. "Can't get these on assistance."

"Really? How can potato chips be okay but not a sandwich or a cup of coffee?"

He shrugged. "Don't make the rules."

Her eyes closed and she conceded through gritted teeth. "Fine." As he pushed keys on the register to readjust the total, Treaz spotted a nearby display boasting cheap wine at less than four dollars. Leaning over, she selected two bottles.

The clerk kept his head down but raised his eyes to her. "Uh, yeah, no alcohol either."

No surprise there. She reached in her pocket for the rest of her money.

"You still want the dog and—"

"Just the chips. And the wine."

Saying nothing further, he bagged up her purchases. She staggered out of the shop with seventeen cents left to her name.

"Damn you, Pearl Man," she complained. A woman hurried past with her face turned away. Treaz realized she wasn't only thinking a stream of curses about her boss, but talking out loud. She laughed hysterically. "Listen to me. I really am a crazy person." A couple crossed the street to avoid her. "Hey," she yelled. "You think I'm gonna hurt you?"

Back at the bus stop, Treaz unscrewed the first wine bottle and consumed it along with the state approved junk food. She mumbled to herself for twenty-five minutes, alternating between laughing and crying. No one came close. Her bus finally squealed to a stop, and she climbed aboard. Fumbling, she got out her pass and ran it through the machine. There was a beep.

"Not enough, ma'am," said the driver without emotion.

"That can't be. I've only used it once." She tried again, still no good.

The driver glanced at his cell phone. "You got cash?"

Treaz held out her dime, nickel, and two pennies.

He shook his head. "Gotta get off."

She stared at him. "Please, I need to get home."

He looked at his watch and motioned her off. "Ma'am, you need to exit now or I have to call this in. Got a schedule to keep."

She stepped from the bus, the doors whooshed shut, and her ride drove off. Unbelievable. How could things get any worse? If only Pearl Man had given her a phone number or some way to reach him. She lost track of how long it took to find her way back to Zoe's awful place. It was dark, and she was sobering up. She noticed that where she lived was actually a rent-by-the-week motel, not an apartment building. It stood in an area surrounded by barred-windowed and graffiti-covered buildings.

Panting, she trudged up the steps. All she wanted was to lie down on that filthy mattress. Who cared if her rat roommate was home or not.

"Zoe," came a gruff voice.

Treaz turned to a short, stubby man with scratched glasses and a strong odor of garlic. "I'm not telling you again. You either pay up or you're out of here tomorrow."

She sighed. Her whole life felt like a scene from a bad movie. "I just need a few more days."

The landlord placed a finger in his ear and wiggled it.

"Please. The employment office has work for me soon," she fibbed. Surely, she could find something on her own by then.

"By 6:00 am, or you're out."

She lifted her hands. "What do you want me to do? Go turn tricks?"

"Whatever it takes."

Treaz was too tired to be appalled. She was no prostitute, but couldn't speak for Zoe.

The landlord pointed at the bottle in her paper bag. His face balled up. "You're just a no good drunk."

"I am not."

"You got 'til 6:00 am, or I'll call the police. Or better yet, your parole officer." He stomped down the stairs. "I hate this job."

"Not as much as I hate mine," she screamed back. "I should report you to the authorities. Living in some back alley would be better than these horrid conditions. It's not worth one single dollar to live here." It didn't seem to matter what she said. How sad that this Zoe woman existed in this utter hopelessness and despair every day.

When Treaz entered her room, she shivered. She turned on the heat, but only cold air blew out. Not able to stand the smell of Zoe's clothes anymore, she stripped everything off. Her foot caught in the jeans, and she tumbled to the ground. Blood gushed from her knee, cut open from a discarded can on the floor. "Why are you such a slob, Zoe?" Now she'd probably need a tetanus shot. Finding no bandaids, she blotted her wound with toilet paper. It became a sticky mess. Refusing to use the disgusting, moldy shower, she wet one of the unlaundered towels to clean up the best she could. Treaz put on yoga pants and a long-

164

sleeved shirt. The garments still reeked, yet not as bad, or she was growing accustomed to the stench.

Sitting in the center of the lumpy mattress, tears streamed down her cheeks. How in the world was she supposed to help anyone while in this Host body? Pearl Man was an unbelievably insensitive man. He didn't care about her, and she hated him.

In the dull illumination of the overhead light, she saw a solo beady eye watching. Her furry roommate huddled in the corner. At least HE hadn't abandoned her. Treaz broke the seal on the second bottle and drank most of the wine while wrapped within the urine-smelling blanket. Before finishing it, she threw up by the side of the bed and passed out.

22

OMANI

The day dragged on for Omani as she oriented a new maintenance employee, dealt with broken vacuum cleaners, and conducted quality checks in several offices. She couldn't wait until the evening when she would send her message out—her first attempt at finding an online friend.

Mid-way through the afternoon, Omani grabbed some time to herself. She fixed a cup of hot chocolate and went to sit outside. As she huddled close to one of the heaters, she thought about Franklin. She hoped to find someone as likable as he'd been when she was just sixteen. Omani recalled her last few conversations with him. She had hurried through all her homework and studying, ate dinner with her mother, and done up all the supper dishes. After what felt like an eternity, but was only two minutes, Franklin replied.

OL: Franklin, Franklin, Franklin!

FM: What's up, Miss Omani?

OL: MOM AND I ARE COMING TO AMERICA! Eek, I'm so excited!

FM: That is exciting. You've been wanting to do that for awhile.

OL: Just for forever. It's not gonna be until next year in October. For twenty whole days!

FM: My birthday month.

OL: Really? I've been trying to convince my mom that we should come visit you. It would be so cool to meet you in person.

There was a long delay and Omani looked at the clock. Their nightly fifteen minute chats passed quickly, so she hated when Franklin didn't respond immediately. Thirty seconds past.

OL: You still there? Can we come?

FM: Oh honey, I don't think that will work.

Omani frowned. Whenever Franklin used the word 'honey', it usually was followed with something parental.

OL: That's what my mom said, too. But I don't get why.

FM: Because I'm so busy with my job.

OL: You can't take like one day off? There's got to be a way. You work from home, so we could come to your house.

FM: No. I'm sorry, Omani. Not a good idea, either. My wife wouldn't understand. Somehow, I'm always in trouble with her.

Omani slumped back in her chair. What's the big deal? Why was his wife so naggy and mean?

FM: I want you both to have a great time. You can tell me about everything when you return, OK?

OL: Yeah, I will.

Suddenly, she had an idea. A fantastic one. Only two more minutes remained before they had to sign off.

OL: If I can't see you, at least I could deliver you a birthday present.

FM: No need.

OL: If your wife will be mad about that too, I'll just leave it in a secret place, and you can go find it.

FM: Are you sure you're even coming to Arizona?

OL: Mom said we are. I'll find the perfect spot and tell you where it'll be.

FM: That's not necessary.

OL: You won't change my mind. I'll figure everything out and pick a place only you can find.

FM: You'd need to wrap everything tight in case it rains.

OL: I will.

FM: What's it going to be?

OL: I can't tell you, silly. Otherwise, there'd be no surprise.

The next morning, Omani explained her plans to her mother. Hanna tried to talk her out of the idea by explaining they were going to the Grand Canyon in northern Arizona.

"Franklin lives in Phoenix which is several hours away. Maybe we could make arrangements for next time."

"Like in forty years or something?"

Her mother laughed. "So dramatic, Ani."

"Seriously. Franklin's our friend. Please?"

Hanna relented. "What do you intend to leave for him?"

"I gotta think about it. Small stuff for sure. Definitely some photographs of us, since we can't send those through your special messaging thing."

"I'm sure he'll appreciate anything. I'd love to see what you box up before you seal it," she said.

Omani walked to the office door, then turned back. "Mom, Franklin's wife is kinda awful, don't you think? Why would she be upset at him about us?"

Her mother waggled her finger. "We shouldn't assume. We've never met her."

"I hope someday we can meet Franklin in person. Maybe he'll come here—without his wife."

"Don't be late for school, love."

That night, Omani explored Google Earth to search around Franklin's home town. She found a location about a mile from his house. She zoomed in close on a clump of newly planted trees and shrubs near the back of a park. Now to find the right container.

Omani drank the last of her now cold hot chocolate. Not long after that conversation everything had turned bad, thanks to Uncle Filip. He ruined everything. So often she had wondered if her gift ever even made it to Franklin.

Omani returned to her room at the end of the day. She went straight to her computer and switched it on. Her thoughts went to Franklin. He had been such a wonderful friend for a teenager. He likely wouldn't be around any longer, but she anticipated finding a new friend just as wonderful.

She pulled up the options on her private server, hovering over the word External, yet stopped before clicking. Omani knew she could easily register with one of the online Friend Services she scoped out, but what would happen if she tried something else? Might she get another result?

Instead of selecting External, she clicked on the word Comm. Up popped a screen with a blinking cursor. She hesitated, her heart pounding. Filip employed people to monitor everything. This would be a true test of Rafael's skills and if he was able to keep things under wraps, otherwise everything would fall apart. Omani had to trust him.

She rubbed her hands together and, as Franklin originally did, she typed one word, in English. When still a child, she learned that was the universal language, but more importantly, it was how she'd communicated with Franklin.

OL: Hello?

For thirty minutes she sat staring at her screen. She half-expected a knock at her door from Elias. With no response and no unwanted visitors, Omani went to the bathroom and got ready for bed. She hoped it wouldn't take seven years to receive a reply, like her mother had waited.

She checked again, no message. Rafael had told her not to go into anything besides the internet browser. Perhaps he'd done the programming so nothing else would work. She stared and lingered awhile longer.

OL: Hello?

A simple five letter word that might change her life, or not. Another twenty minutes passed. Omani sighed. If nothing came within a week or two, she would return to the internet to find someone, although that wasn't what she wanted. She longed for someone interesting, entertaining, and more adventurous.

She must be patient.

23

TREAZ

Treaz woke with a pounding headache. And naked. Thank God. Who had been her Asset? Garry the bartender? She hoped this next Host would be some rich person with a lavish lifestyle and clean clothes. It didn't take long before the same foul smell assaulted her nose, and she bolted upright. Still Zoe. Treaz fell back in the bed. Had she the energy to endure another day in this body? Vaguely she remembered waking up in the night sweating, and stripping off her clothes. The heater must have kicked in.

Examining her wounded knee, she saw bits of white toilet paper and towel lint mixed in with the dried blood. Her eyes stared at the ceiling fan overhead. It made a low repetitive grinding as the lopsided faux wood slats turned. Three of the four bulbs were burned out. A mass of fire engines and ambulances roared past the building with their sirens blaring. She covered her ears and massaged her temples, purposely turning away from the disgusting mess of vomit on the floor, the result of excessive potato chips and cheap red wine. Treaz had heard drinking more alcohol helped alleviate a hangover. Isn't that why bloody mary's were invented? Hair of the dog or something. The nearby bottle still contained a last serving. Should she try it? Anything would be better than the throb, throb, throb in her head.

A sharp knock came on the front door. She didn't move. The knock repeated, harder. Slowly getting to her feet, she shuffled over to open the door.

"Jesus, Zoe. Put some clothes on," said the landlord turning away.

Treaz looked down at her nakedness, not caring. It wasn't her body. She reached for some pants and a shirt from a pile. "Do you have any asp—"

"You need to leave," he said coldly.

"But—"

"Don't tempt me to make any calls. Get your stuff and get out. You've got ten minutes."

She wanted to cry, scream, die. "Where am I supposed to go?"

"Not my problem."

"I don't have—"

The man lifted his arm. "Out."

How heartless could he be? She slammed the door in his face. Where was she to go? She had no home, no money, no friend, no job, nothing! Pearl Man didn't care. He'd given up, condemning her to be Zoe forever.

Finding a grocery bag, she put in the final two cans of soup and crackers, and shoved in a few articles of clothing. The plastic broke, spewing everything to the floor. She cried in frustration, then saw Pearl Man's cardboard box. She despised that man.

Her landlord leaned against the wall outside her room, arms folded. Treaz sucked in a long breath, held her head high, and brushed past carrying her meager possessions. "You're pitiful," she spat as she descended the stairs and walked down the sidewalk hungry, cold, and unsure where to go.

Treaz wandered for an hour, up and down streets, trying to figure out what to do. People wearing business suits avoided eye-contact. Even the homeless ignored her, shuffling by with their heads down. She felt invisible and miserable.

Resting on a bench across from the federal courthouse, she noticed the attached jail facility with the razor wire atop the walls. Perhaps she could force Pearl Man out of hiding if she was arrested. Inmates were probably treated better. The landlord mentioned a parole officer, and Treaz wondered if Zoe had spent time in a cell.

A growl came from her gut. She looked in the box at one of the two remaining cans. Cold soup would work. Her head fell forward when she realized she'd forgotten to take the can opener. Across the street was an overcrowded café. She went to stand in line to make her request. When she reached the front the hostess frowned. "You can't come in here."

"I just need to borrow a can opener," said Treaz.

The young woman might have been a model with her picture-perfect outfit, fake eyelashes, and flawless red lipstick. She pinched her nostrils and grimaced. "We don't serve vagrants."

Treaz inspected the entrance. "Nothing's posted."

The woman glared. "I said, we don't serve homeless people."

"Why not?" Treaz cocked her head. "A bit judgmental, wouldn't you say? How do you know I'm homeless?"

Antsy, the woman's eyes darted everywhere but at Treaz. Prospective diners lined up, and the hostess feigned a smile at the couple behind Treaz. "Party of two?"

"Hey, I'm right here. Party of one," Treaz said, growing more belligerent. No one should be treated this way. "There's an open seat at the bar."

The woman sneered. "That's the last place you need to be." She motioned for the couple to follow her. They gave Treaz a pathetic look. The hostess seated them and handed out menus, while grinning her red-lipped, fake smile and keeping an eye on Treaz.

Red Lips didn't know if Treaz held a million dollars or seventeen cents in her pocket. She resisted the urge to walk over and smack those perfect lips. Instead she went and sat on the open bar stool.

Soon the hostess strode over, her eyes intense with rage. "You can't stay here."

Treaz didn't move.

"I'm going to call the police."

"Have at it," Treaz said smugly.

"How dare—"

"Whoa," said an approaching server to Red Lips. "Is there a reason why she can't sit here?"

Treaz straightened up her back.

"She's homeless," Red Lips replied.

The man shooed the hostess away. "Go do your frickin' job." The woman gritted her teeth and returned to the front podium. The waiter smiled warmly. "She's a witch who's lost her broom. I'm Kevin."

Her eyes instantly watered at his simple recognition of her existence, regardless of how lousy it was. "Treaz, uh, Zoe."

"Let me get you some water."

The hostess threw daggers with her eyes towards her un-welcomed customer. Treaz smiled back, offering plenty of sweet syrup.

Kevin delivered ice water, a white ceramic plate with a ham and cheese sandwich, french fries, and a dill pickle.

Treaz bit her lip, embarrassed. "I'm sorry. The hostess was right. I don't have any money to pay, well, except for seventeen…"

"My treat."

She swallowed down her emotions and her pride. There *was* a kind soul left in the world. "Thank you," she said, then devoured every bite.

With a full belly, she watched Kevin work. Was he her Asset? Treaz hadn't thought much about her official job beyond cursing her boss. It would be so much simpler if Pearl Man told her who the Asset was rather than making her guess. However, Kevin didn't seem like he needed anything as he was friendly, efficient, and seemed happy with exactly what he was doing.

He grinned as he waved the bill and a twenty wildly in the air so the hostess couldn't miss seeing it, then pushed the money toward Treaz. "You be safe, Treaz-Zoe." Once again, tears filled her eyes as Kevin disappeared to serve new customers, and she tucked the money in her pocket.

Treaz picked up her belongings and went to the restroom to wash up. It wasn't just Zoe's clothes that stank, but her. She hadn't bathed since being in Bella's body. Gross. A thorough sponge bath ensued, followed by slipping into Zoe's sleeveless dress. She yanked extra paper towels from the dispenser and dropped them in her cardboard box hearing her grandmother's voice, "Just in case."

Even though only eleven days had passed since this whole nightmare had begun, Treaz missed Grammie terribly. She longed to feel her old, weakened arms wrap around her and tell her she was home, just like she had done so many times when Treaz was a child and her mother suffered another episode or bout of depression. Treaz was afraid Grammie would be ashamed to see her like this. When she Advanced out of Zoe's body, she would find a way back to San Antonio.

177

Treaz unlocked the door and exited with the box. Three women were waiting, and gave her frustrated looks. She acted like she belonged there.

Later, darkness brought cooling temperatures, and in a gas station restroom, she changed into her last set of clothes, a pair of jeans and a sweat shirt. Treaz slept in the park that night.

24

TREAZ

Treaz sat on a bench watching kids play kickball while she contemplated what to do next. Happy families laughed, enjoying the sunny day. They held no worries that their nice warm houses with stocked refrigerators might not be there when they got home—a home like she used to live in. Grammie's home. How she had taken everything for granted. Treaz went into a McDonalds for an egg muffin and two large coffees. If she skipped eating for the rest of the day, and could find a way to significantly add to Kevin's money, perhaps she'd have enough to get a cheap motel that night. Sleeping on the street again sounded horrific.

She walked to a small gas station, hid her box behind the dumpster, then waited by the corner of the building until a customer wearing a business suit drove in to fill up their tank. Treaz approached slowly. "Hello."

The woman looked up with wary eyes.

"I wondered if maybe you had some spare change?"

The woman shook her head, "Sorry. No."

Treaz nodded and disappeared back behind the building.

When the next patron arrived, she tried again, "Would you have a couple dollars?" The man frowned and turned his back.

How she hated doing this! It was so humiliating. She thought about when she had turned away people asking for money.

The next person she engaged with a different tactic. It was one someone unsuccessfully attempted with her in the past. "Do you have a dollar, twenty-nine cents? I just need a little more to catch a bus home."

She kept trying and her stories became more creative as the day went on. Eventually, the clerk came out and chased her off because someone complained about her pan-handling. Her final take? Six dollars and forty-three cents, nothing close to paying for a room.

Treaz fetched the hidden box and wandered away, not knowing where she would go. Unable to stop herself, she soon was inside a convenience store purchasing a four-pack of single serve wine bottles.

In her old life in San Antonio she'd seen homeless people living beneath overpasses. She went to seek one out for herself. Precariously crawling up into a high nook under a bridge, she sat down with her box. Treaz opened the screw top of the first plastic bottle and drank several swallows as she acknowledged spending most of her collected money on booze—again.

"Zoe, Zoe," she admonished aloud, opening the second wine. By the time she finished the third bottle, despair was settling in. A burning sensation came at the back of her eyes as she started to cry. She rubbed her face and wiped her nose on her already dirty sleeve. Never in her life did she envision being this low, this demoralized, this desperate.

Another woman clambered to Treaz and shooed her away. "This is my spot. You can sleep over there," she said, pointing to an empty corner on the far side.

Without even the energy to argue, Treaz stumbled to her resting place for the night—a hard bed of cement with spider webs draped overhead. There she consumed her fourth serving of alcohol and fell asleep, everything spinning.

25
OMANI

Omani delayed twenty-four hours before finding herself in front of her computer with hands poised on the keys. What could be taking so long to receive a reply? Omani couldn't ask Rafael if he'd set that part up because he didn't know her intentions. Of course her mother had waited a lot longer than her. She hoped this wouldn't be an exchange that took multiple days or years to send and communicate. Her mother always said Omani lacked patience.

She typed another message to whoever might be on the other end, if anybody.

OL: Hello? I'm just saying, hello.

To distract herself, Omani spent an hour *surfing the web* as it used to be called when she was a girl. After enough wasted time, she reached to shut everything down, when a one word response popped up.

IM: Hey.

Omani stared at the single greeting. Her heart thumped, and she shook her hands hard in excitement. Somebody responded!

She recalled when her mother first heard from Franklin and figured she must be feeling the exact same thrill.

She balled up and released her fingers trying to decide what to say next. At first, she entered, "Why didn't you respond right away?" but thought that might come across as rude to begin this potential pen-pal-type relationship. She changed her words.

OL: Hi. Thank you for responding.
IM: Who is this?

A thought struck her. What happened if this was someone in her Uncle's organization? If discovered, she'd lose her computer completely or be given a harsher punishment. Yet, Rafael promised no one would find out. Her enthusiasm outweighed her concern, so she remained optimistically cautious.

OL: You can call me, O. Who is this?
IM: O? Is that a code name or something?

She supposed it was. But, she didn't want to give her proper name yet. Although, if Uncle Filip saw her messages, he probably would figure things out right away.

IM: Are you some kind of spy?
OL: No, nothing like that.
IM: Who do you work for?
OL: My Uncle.

She needed to be mindful until she got a better feel for this person, while at the same time didn't want to scare him or her off.

OL: Don't worry. I'm not one of those hacker people.

Twenty seconds ticked by. Omani consulted the time and fidgeted. She reminded herself that her mother wasn't there telling her she could only chat for fifteen minutes.

IM: Hacker people?
OL: People who break into computers and do bad things like stealing and sabotage.

Her definition was far from effective. Yet she did hold a little pride that at least she knew about hacking now, thanks to the textbooks from Rafael.

IM: How'd you get here? Why aren't your messages encrypted?

She remembered reading about encryption as well.

OL: I don't know how to do that. I had someone I trust set this up so no one could read our messages.
IM: Who would be looking?

She coached herself. "Stay generic. Re-direct the conversation."

OL: I just have to be careful. What's your name?

There was another pause. Was he deciding to tell her?

IM: Iggy. Like in Iggy Pop.
OL: Who's that?
IM: Dude, you never heard of Iggy Pop?

Omani widened her eyes. Dude?

OL: I'm not a dude. I'm a woman.

IM: Sorry, O. I didn't know. I'm a guy, by the way.

OL: That's alright. So Iggy, why didn't you respond to my first message?

IM: I wasn't sure if it was a trap or not. In fact, maybe it still is.

OL: No, it isn't. I promise.

IM: Hold on a sec.

Omani held for a couple minutes, then Iggy continued.

IM: Work stuff.

OL: What do you do?

IM: I'm in the communications business. You?

OL: I oversee all the kitchen, maintenance, and housekeeping duties for a large facility. We've got about seventy-five people who live and work here.

IM: 🙂

The smiley face emoji brought on a chuckle. She hadn't seen one of those since she was a kid. Iggy appeared to be loosening up a bit.

IM: So, how come you messaged me?

Omani wondered what she should tell him. Should she be honest? He seemed trustworthy, and no one had come breaking down her door.

186

OL: I wanted to talk with someone. :)   (I can't do the emoji's on my computer. I have to do the old fashioned version.)

She laughed at her own playfulness. It felt good.

OL: And, who is Iggy Pop?

Nothing for a full minute.

IM: O, I gotta run.

Iggy probably had a social life, unlike her. Or he had a boss peering over his shoulder. Maybe *he* was the boss.

OL: Sure. I hope we can chat again.

No more messages came and she found herself disappointed, yet her efforts to find someone had worked, at least so far. She enjoyed her brief interaction with Iggy, and could envision them possibly becoming real online friends. So many questions swirled in her mind of things they'd discuss. Oh! She forgot to even ask where he lived. Next time.

26
TREAZ

Treaz's restless night ended with a stiff back and the glare of a bright sunrise in her eyes. Between her thighs was a familiar warmth. She touched the wetness and saw blood on her pants. Her eyes watered. Could things get any worse?

Behind a bush, she changed back into the dress, placing the stash of scratchy paper towels inside her soiled underwear. Treaz needed a proper solution, so she walked until finding a small church. After pounding on the locked door, a woman opened it slightly and directed her to a facility a mile away.

She joined the queue of people waiting outside the location. For thirty-five minutes she jostled among the other unkept smelly bodies until she made it to the counter. Treaz received her portion and sat down at a long table. She gobbled down a peanut butter jelly sandwich and bowl of soup while the man next to her kept eyeing her food. Worsening cramps pushed her to address her other issue which was becoming a problem. She went to find someone to explain her predicament.

The helpful volunteer provided some pads and showed her to the bathroom. The stalls were barely big enough to move in, so Treaz left her box of possessions on the floor outside the door and got herself cleaned up. When she opened the stall, her box was gone.

"Hey, who took my stuff?" she asked the woman who was washing her face in the sink. The woman shrugged her shoulders. "Seriously, you didn't see anyone walk out of here with a cardboard box?"

Treaz emerged from the restroom, and found one of the volunteers to lodge her complaint. "Somebody stole my things."

The woman exhaled and forced a half-smile. "Alright. Let's take a look around."

Treaz knew it was hopeless. Everything she had in the world was now gone, including Kevin's remaining money. She should have never left her box out of her sight. Tears of defeat welled in her eyes. "Never mind," she told the volunteer, and left the building. For years Treaz donated cans of food at Thanksgiving time to help those less fortunate. Her assumption that shelters were a place of refuge were now dashed. Things were not as rosy and wonderful as all that.

During her journey to nowhere, she managed to find a handful of people to give her a few dollars each. Maybe she did have an influential gene after all, like Pearl Man talked about. She earned enough to buy herself another four pack of wine and took long swigs to activate the high as quickly as possible, hoping to alleviate her emotional pain.

Treaz walked along a road overlooking the freeway beneath. As the cars raced past she thought about how naive she had been about the homeless and how she usually ignored them. Shame overwhelmed her. She deserved to be there.

She lamented over the lost sleeping pills, which she wanted to take in one last gulp to eliminate her misery. She drank more. Perhaps she could drink herself to death. Nobody would know of Treaz Popa. They would only find Zoe Landis. Awkwardly, she crawled over the guardrail. Keeping only a light grip, she leaned against the railing. "Oh, she was just a drunk," people would say. If she jumped, it would serve Pearl Man right to lose his *special* Transitioner. Nothing would come from this situation. She would never see Grammie again anyway. Her life could never be the same.

Treaz—Zoe teetered on the edge as traffic rushed by thirty feet below.

Echoed voices were heard, but not clear. Was she still Zoe? Had she Advanced? Could she be back in her own body?

She tried to lift her arm, but again she was restrained. Treaz managed to open her eyes, squinting at the bright overhead light. She lay in a hospital bed surrounded by blue drapes. An IV was inserted in the back of her left hand.

"You feeling better, Zoe?" said a nurse entering the curtains and putting a clip onto Treaz's index finger. "You're in St. Joseph's. You were running low on a few things, but you're on the mend now." She pointed at the IV. "You've been receiving some needed fluids. My name's Collette."

"Can you take these restraints off?" Treaz asked, not liking the anxiousness growing in her belly.

Collette removed the bands. "You were a little combative when you arrived."

Treaz's memory was fuzzy. "How'd I get here?"

"Some good Samaritan brought you in saying you were disoriented." Collette raised the head of the bed. "They found you under a tree at one of the downtown parks."

Treaz exhaled. "Did that good Samaritan happen to have a pearl earring?"

"Have no idea." Collette filled a cup with water. "A social worker is coming to visit you as well as someone to collect your insurance information."

Did Zoe even have any kind of insurance? Maybe a government program? "I'd like to just have my clothes and go home," Treaz said.

The nurse scrunched her nose, "It's policy. If you're having some anxiety, I can talk with the doctor about prescribing some medication."

"I'm fine," Treaz lied. Her face felt tingly, but the remembrance of what happened in the psych ward while in Danielle's body scared her from accepting any more pills. "After I talk to that person, can I be released?"

"You don't have any injuries, but they will assess your situation and make the final decision, along with your physician."

"When will they be in?"

Collette consulted her watch, "Probably within an hour. You up to eating something? I can call down to the cafeteria for some lunch."

"Sure. That would be nice. Maybe a sandwich I can take with me?"

"Alright hun, I'll put in the order. If you need something else, use the button here," and she gave Treaz a handheld pad with a red nurse icon on it. "Don't get out of bed by yourself."

"Okay."

After Collette left, Treaz swung her legs off the bed and got down to the floor. There was no way she was staying in that hospital ten more minutes. Her body felt shaky, but she must deal with it. Looking at her hand, she took ahold of the IV. She hated anything to do with tubes and needles, but it had to be removed. Tugging off the extremely sticky tape, the red plastic tube slipped right out with only a drop of blood and a little sting. Under the bed she found her smelly dress neatly folded. She considered wearing the clean gown, but knew that would be a dead giveaway, so she dressed and put her shoes back on.

Poking her head out, Treaz watched Collette hurry through another curtain. There seemed to be some commotion happening —the perfect distraction to make her escape. She moved quickly passed a desk where another nurse focused on a computer. On the way to the exit, she confiscated a handful of tampons from a janitor's cart.

Once in the daylight, she shaded her eyes. Here she was again, out on the street. Treaz went to rest for a while at a nearby park. A woman chatting on her cell phone sat at the opposite end of the bench. In a small sandy area, a girl about five years old, played on the slide.

As the mother continued talking, the little girl skipped up and snuggled close to her mom. Treaz could feel the girl staring, so she turned and gave her a smile. The child waved a tiny hand, then tapped her mother's arm. "Mommy?" Her mother brushed her daughter's hand away and kept talking.

The girl grinned again, and Treaz winked back. "Mommy?" She pulled at her mother's sleeve.

"Not now. I'm on the phone," the mother whispered, irritated. But the girl stayed persistent. The mother finally became frustrated and ended her call. "I gotta go. I'll talk to you later." Then she glared at her daughter. "What?"

"Can we give that nice lady some of my fishy crackers? I've got lots extra."

Her mother looked up and witnessed Treaz for the first time. Horrified, she stood and grabbed ahold of her child's hand. As the girl was yanked away, she received a scolding. "No. We don't give things to strangers. I told you that before." The girl waved farewell to Treaz who reciprocated.

"And that's how we learn," said Treaz. She saw Pearl Man approaching, but didn't have the energy for anger. "Were you my good Samaritan?" He sat down. Treaz rubbed her temples. "I can't even kill myself without you interfering."

He put his hand reassuringly on her shoulder. "Treaz. I would never want anything bad to happen to you."

She scoffed. "Yeah. It might reflect in your employee retention stats."

He shook his head. "Think, Treaz. Zoe must be an alcoholic. Since she's your Host body, you will experience those tendencies as well."

Treaz closed her eyes in a wave of relief and surprise. Of course, that made sense. She did drink, but not obsessively like Zoe. "Why can't I overcome that? I'm not her."

"Sometimes it just feels so natural, it isn't apparent. Fight off the craving. Think like Treaz. Keep sober and do what's needed to Advance as soon as possible."

"Can't you just take me off this assignment?"

He lowered his hand. "You must finish. Think of your assignment as a gift."

Treaz sighed. While a child, whenever she struggled with difficult homework and would whine and complain, her grandmother always told her, "Accept your assignment as a gift from God. You can always find a lesson to learn." Treaz was pretty sure that English reports and social study exercises were not a present from the Divine. And certainly these Vanguard assignments were not a favor from above. Yet, maybe there was something to learn from her Host body. Could Zoe teach her something? She already had.

Pearl Man handed her a twenty dollar bill.

"That's it?" She asked.

"That's it. You've got work to do."

27

TREAZ

Treaz used a little of Pearl Man's money for a cheap, fast food meal. Nothing healthy, but enough to thwart the growling. Experiencing Zoe's urge to purchase more wine, she fought off the temptation and walked by the liquor store.

With no destination in mind but the need to stay busy, she wandered for three hours up and down roads, through parks, and past homes and apartments. She went to investigate a massive stone building that intrigued her.

Standing before a branch of the Phoenix library, she wondered if she could find out anything useful about Vanguard, like who ran it and what their goals might be. Influencing random people to make certain decisions didn't seem very productive. Case in point, take Beckman. If he took Treaz's advice and went back to school, or built his app, surely that would take years to accomplish. What was Vanguard planning to achieve? Perhaps she would find some insights about Transitioning and Assets and Counselors. The whole outfit must be totally illegal, so she might find nothing at all.

Treaz entered the doors and stood looking for the computer area. A woman approached from behind and quietly, yet urgently, asked if they might have a word outside.

Here we go again—disrespect and handled like a second class citizen.

"I hate to embarrass you inside," said the woman, "but you can't come in looking like you do."

A man of about seventy with thick glasses stopped ten feet away to witness their exchange.

"You are a community service, right?" asked Treaz.

"Yes, but—"

"I'm a part of this community. So what's the problem?"

The employee searched for words. "It's disruptive to our other guests."

"All I did was walk through the door."

"I realize that, but you're—"

"I'm what? Dirty and smelly?"

The woman grimaced and nodded.

Treaz glanced over at the gentleman watching. Embarrassed and demoralized, she looked back to the clerk. "Well, I'm sorry I don't fit your screening process. Did you ask everyone else sitting in the library if they showered and brushed their teeth this morning?"

Blowing out a breath, the woman cast her eyes to the ground. "I've been told that I—"

"Can't let a homeless person in." Treaz scratched her head hoping she hadn't picked up the worst ever lice from somewhere. "I have a library card and pay my taxes." Yet, she doubted both those assumptions for Zoe.

The woman tilted her head. "I apologize. Maybe you could come back another time."

A knot tied in Treaz's stomach. She ought to offer up some choice words, and barge inside anyway. Who cared if people were offended by her presence? She had just as much right to be there as anyone else. "And if I refuse to leave?"

"Please, don't make me call the police."

She'd had enough humiliation. Treaz turned away. "Whatever, lady."

After the woman went back inside, the older man shook his head and followed her.

They may be able to keep Treaz out of the building, but they couldn't stop her from sitting on public property! She slid down a wall, stunned at the rudeness of some people. Had Zoe's bad choices resulted in her downfall, or had she been a product of crappy luck and an unhelpful system? She sat with her legs stretched out in front of her. The extra-large coke from earlier might have provided a temporary sugar high, but it was not helping with the ensuing headache.

Mired in her thoughts, she disregarded the people entering and exiting. Then, a bottle of water appeared before her face, and she looked up to the man with the glasses who had stopped to listen to the earlier altercation.

"Thought you might enjoy this. That woman was rude, and I told her so."

Treaz accepted the cold water. "She was just doing her job."

"Still, it's a ridiculous policy," he said. "You mind if I sit with you?"

That surprised her. "Sure."

He handed the three books he was holding to her, then awkwardly got down on the ground with a grunt and a chuckle. "Haven't been down here for a while. My name is Richard Jenkens." He reached out and they shook hands.

"Treaz."

"Nice to meet you."

She returned his books. "What are you reading?"

Richard set the well-used hardbacks down. "Oh, a little Tolstoy and Twain. Been re-reading all the classics since my wife died."

"I'm sorry for your loss. How long ago?"

"Four months, sixteen days." He smiled, even as his eyes watered. "You want me to add the hours?"

Treaz opened the water bottle and slowly drank half down. She saw how the old man was hurting, and she thought about her Grammie.

He motioned to her. "You have family?"

She sighed. "My mom got ill when I was just nine, so I moved in with my grandmother. When I was twelve, my mother passed away."

Richard nodded. "Are your grandparents still with you? Aunts or uncles?"

"My Grammie's still alive." Treaz hoped that was the case, but Grammie had not seemed so well the last time Treaz visited. That felt like years ago now, but in reality had only been weeks. "She made my life bearable, and even put me through college."

"Sounds like she has quite an impact on you."

Treaz smiled. "She is intelligent and funny and always telling me stories of when she grew up."

Richard laughed. "Us ancients are masterful storytellers, or at least we think we are."

"I absolutely cherish my Grammie."

"Why are you not staying with her now?"

"She has dementia. I was forced to move her into a home for full-time care." She sat silent for a few moments.

Richard said nothing. After a minute, he readjusted his position on the cement. "I spent some time on the streets myself before I was married."

Her eyes widened. "You did? Where?"

"Right here in Phoenix. For almost a year."

"What happened?"

Richard pushed his glasses farther up his nose. "Gambled on a business that failed."

"Oh, no."

He waved his hand in dismissal. "That was a long time ago. How about you, Treaz? How'd you end up in this predicament?"

She consumed more water giving her time to decide how to answer his question, unsure if she should say anything that in fact, she shouldn't. Of course, speaking as Zoe, it was easier to imagine. "I drink too much and can't hold down a job. Got kicked out of my apartment three days ago."

He nodded as if he understood completely without passing any judgment.

Treaz and Richard engaged in a pleasant conversation for almost an hour about treasured authors, types of music, hobbies they each wished they'd started. He told her about his late wife's cooking and her free-spirited knitting group. They were never blessed with children, and he was the only remaining sibling from his family. Talking to Richard was like spending time with a favorite grandpa, one with a soft belly that a kid loved to snuggle against and fall asleep.

"I'm alone, now, except for my stories," he said patting the stack next to him. "I suppose I'm waiting to go be with my wife."

Treaz could think of nothing to say. What a beautiful relationship she hoped to experience if she could only get back in her own body.

He changed topics, nodding at the library. "Were you looking for something in particular?"

"I wanted to research an organization."

"One you want to work for?"

All that was too complicated to explain. "Maybe."

Richard began to stand. "I ought to get on home, now. Hard to see in the dark anymore."

Treaz jumped up and helped him to his feet. "I enjoyed talking with you." She didn't want him to leave.

"I did as well." Then he embraced her with a strong hug, like a child might give to a lost teddy bear after being found.

She almost cried. He didn't care how much she smelled or how filthy she was. Whether lice infested her hair, or she bothered to brush her teeth. Her eyes closed as he squeezed her tight.

"I have a deal to make with you," he whispered in her ear.

"Of course," she said, and he released her.

Richard pulled out his wallet. Though she needed money, she didn't want to take it from that man. "I can't—"

"Please," he insisted pushing three hundred dollars into her hands. "Sleep in a hotel for a couple nights. Take some long hot baths—like my wife did every night. Buy yourself some new clothes and a few decent meals. I would like you to meet me here the day after tomorrow at noon, so we can do your research. They're not open on New Year's Day."

"Why are you doing this?" she asked, her throat constricting.

"Because I sense a beautiful but lost soul." She hugged him again. "I am trusting that you won't spend it on alcohol."

"I won't, I promise," she assured him as she stuffed the money tightly in her front pocket. "Thank you, Richard."

He nodded. "Treaz is a lovely, unusual name."

"My real name is Nadia, but Grammie always called me Treaz."

"Is there a special meaning behind it?"

"I don't know."

He grinned. "Perhaps we can research that as well."

200

She nodded, still shocked at his generosity and kindness towards her.

"See you soon then. Goodnight." Richard waved as he walked away.

"Goodnight." Treaz took in and released a long breath. She watched him until he was out of sight.

28

OMANI

Omani justified her light-hearted mood to finding someone to chat with who didn't live on her Uncle's property. Night couldn't come fast enough when she would send him another message. Hopefully Iggy would not tire of her questions and deem her a pest. She looked out of her window. The dawn's blues and yellows reflected gloriously off the snow-covered mountainside. Even though she hated being stuck there, she never tired of the beauty.

Her day would be busy finalizing the spring planting guides. She loved deciding on flower colors and complimentary foliage. She wanted to discuss with the lead groundskeeper plans for adding new walking paths, and a couple small fountains with nearby shade trees. Uncle Filip didn't care that Omani directed the workers to maintain elegant and stunning grounds, as long as she didn't exceed her budget. In fact, few people paid much attention to her work, but, once in a while, someone would recognize her efforts. It didn't matter, though, because Omani liked it.

After dinner, she retired to her room as a howling winter storm clobbered Vanguard's buildings. Omani paid no attention and hoped her new friend, Iggy, was available.

OL: Hello, Iggy?
IM: Yo, O. Whatsup?

She smiled, and tried to peg his age with his odd and seemingly casual language. Who cared if he was younger—they would never be more than friends. It would be fantastic to actually call and talk to him, but that was impossible. Uncle Filip had security monitoring all calls. They would discover right away Omani had contact with the outside world, and she didn't want to lose what she'd just gained.

OL: Greetings. I hope you are well.
IM: Just peachy.
OL: I wanted to ask where you live.
IM: Hang on.

Omani waited for a minute. She remembered from last time that he had minor work interruptions.

IM: I'm in a small town in the good ole U.S. of A. 🇺🇸

OL: Really? Years ago I knew someone from America, but we lost touch.

IM: You speak…well type English perfectly. Or, you've found some fancy translation app.

OL: It's all me. My mother taught me it's the universal language.

IM: 👍 How about you? Where is your humble home?

She sighed, glancing around her modest room located inside the massive facility.

OL: I'm in Switzerland.

IM: Cool-io! I've never been there but always wanted to snowboard the Alps. The pictures look amazing.

OL: It is gorgeous. I live near the mountains. We have lots of open space.

IM: Sounds awesome. Any sweet slopes close by?

OL: I don't know.

IM: You're not a snowboarder, huh?

Omani raised her brows as she stared at her legs—the ones on which Uncle Filip refused to allow the promised proper surgery when she had finally reached eighteen years old.

OL: Unfortunately not.

IM: Too bad. It's pretty dope. You ever been to my fine country?

Dope? Like in marijuana? Sometimes his word choices were confusing. She hesitated before typing her response.

OL: No. I can't leave the Compound.

IM: What? A Compound? Why not?

Omani balled up her hands thinking about how to best describe things. Should she be honest about her situation? What could it hurt?

OL: Because of the terrorist threat towards me.

There was a pause before Iggy's response. She chewed on her lip as she waited.

IM: Are you just a wee bit paranoid, O?

OL: I'm not scared. That would be my Uncle.

IM: So your Uncle's a hyper paranoid. Why would he think you're in danger? I mean, you do live in Switzerland. Isn't that place the epitome of neutrality?

OL: My Uncle fights terrorism. I think.

Omani wanted to change the subject.

OL: Tell me about your family.

IM: Standard story these days. Dad started out as a happy young man who met a pretty young girl. They fell in love, married, and had a beautiful daughter. Then, pretty young wife ditched unhappy young man a few years later. As a day-trader in the stock market, my dad spent every hour with his head buried in his computer. He never ventured far from the house, from what I heard.

Goodness. Stuck at home, like me; except I have a huge Compound to wander around on.

IM: Eventually, he married my mother and I came along. Pops just repelled excitement in his life, so Mom left him as well. That was my daddy-O…no pun intended.

Omani typed a smiley face using a colon and parenthesis.

IM: After he retired, he promptly died.

OL: That's awful. I'm sorry.

IM: Yup. Goes to show ya'. You gotta live life while you got blood pumping through your veins.

OL: Do you visit your mother and sister?

IM: Nah. Since I was a later-in-life baby, I didn't grow up with my half-sister. I'm like eighteen years younger than her, so we don't have much in common.

OL: And your mother?

IM: Eh, once in a while we talk on the phone. She lives across the country. We haven't seen each other for years.

Omani sighed. She would do anything to spend even five minutes with her own mother again. She couldn't help but prod him.

OL: You should go see your mom, Iggy.

IM: Did she put you up to this?

Her phone buzzed and she glanced at the caller. It was the kitchen number and she ignored it.

OL: Of course not, but making time for family is important. A privilege.

IM: You sound like a mother.

A long-past, familiar aching twisted in her gut. For many years, she wished to have a child of her own to teach and nurture and love. Yet that simply was never a viable possibility in her situation. "Don't preach," she muttered to herself.

OL: Sorry.

IM: So, I told you the sordid tale of my fam. 🙄 How 'bout you?

Her story would take quite a bit longer to tell, and she honestly wasn't up to sharing it then.

OL: Let's leave that until next time. You have fun plans for New Year's Eve?

IM: Nah. Staying in with the pooches. They get freaked out with all the fireworks. Planning an extravagant party at your place?

Omani's phone vibrated again, and she answered it, irritated about the interruption. "What?" Disagreement in the kitchen. She exhaled. "Alright, I'm on my way."

OL: Never. My Uncle's not into celebrating much of anything. Hey, I'm sorry but there's a crisis in the kitchen. I must go.

IM: Check that. L8er, O.

Omani stared at the screen for a few moments before figuring out his farewell bidding. Smiling, she switched everything off, and headed to solve another argument between the cooks that Fritter apparently couldn't handle.

After resolving the issue with no one quitting, Omani returned to her room and lay in bed. Could Filip's anti-terrorism work tie into Iggy's communications job? It did sort of make sense, since Rafael claimed he utilized Vanguard's server to set things up. Was her access truly private? But if it wasn't, her messaging with Iggy would have been discovered by now. Nothing had happened, and no one said anything, so she felt certain everything remained confidential.

Perhaps the Comm sent encrypted messages through to Iggy to foil acts of terror that her Uncle continued to claim were initially orchestrated by Omani's mother. She always struggled to imagine her mother capable of being a terrorist or of being entangled in such horrible deeds. More probable was that her mother would have been trying to stop them like, or unlike, Uncle Filip.

If poor Iggy didn't know he was working for her Uncle, then he was an innocent employee doing his job without understanding what was going on, although, she didn't know either. Regardless, Omani did not want to get him in trouble. Iggy was her friend, so she must keep their conversations benign and not try to push anything forward that might endanger him. Then again, maybe he had no connection to Vanguard at all, and just happened to be on the other end of the line, so to speak. He did say he lived in a small town.

The next evening, she would tell Iggy about her family. It had been a long time since she'd told someone anything about her mother's death. In fact, she couldn't recall if she ever really explained it all.

29

TREAZ

Treaz set up a plan to make the money from Richard last for two days. Her cash needed to be used wisely and not splurged. She planned to go to a hotel she'd seen during her walking that guaranteed low rates and full amenities. But, if she didn't buy different clothing first, she might be rejected from the establishment, so Treaz headed to the Salvation Army.

Looking through the racks of clothes she realized the only time she'd stepped into a thrift store was while searching for a Halloween costume in junior high school. Grammie always took her to either upscale places or boutique type stores. After Treaz grew up, her grandmother still insisted on shopping at expensive retailers. When it came time for newer, more chic attire, Treaz donated her old ones. They likely ended up in a place like this.

If Grammie saw her purchasing used clothing, designer or not, she would not approve. Yet, Treaz wanted to stay under her budget. She exited with a plain blue, long-sleeved dress, comfortable shoes, underclothes, and a pair of jeans and a top all for just under thirty-five dollars. Inside a gas station restroom, she changed and washed her face, and attempted to smooth her hair that was looking like a home for the one-eyed rat in Zoe's previous apartment.

Her preparation worked. When she entered the lobby, there was no problem getting a room on the second floor with a king-sized bed, a heater that she cranked to the hottest temperature, and a bathtub. As Richard suggested, she filled the under-sized tub with steaming water. There were two mini-bottles of shampoo, so she squirted one entirely under the running water to make her own bubbles. She laughed at how tall the fluffy, light billows became, and, when stepping in, how they toppled to the floor. Treaz didn't care. The water kept escaping through the overflow drain, so using her feet, she held a washcloth over the opening. The heat made her skin itch.

Richard was an angel. He looked past her unlovable exterior and didn't speak out of obligation, but like he honestly understood. What a comfort he was in this whole mess. Both he and her grandmother were good storytellers. Treaz remembered curling up against Grammie, with her faint, sweet smell of Joy, to listen. One old story popped into Treaz's mind as she lay soaking.

There once was a poor, young girl named Sofia who lived in a cardboard box on the outskirts of a grand city decorated with emeralds and rubies. The girl led her blind mother each day to the gates to beg for food and money. Sofia longed to live the life of the rich who walked by. She dreamed of filling her tummy with cakes and oranges, bathing in clean water every night, and snuggling into a dry, soft bed.

One day, a woman stopped. Mesmerized by her beauty, Sofia accepted the woman's offer to be her mother, and give her a life in the city. Happily, the girl went along leaving her own mother behind, but soon she was forced to work sixteen hours a day in a hot kitchen scrubbing pots and pans. After ten years, the woman finally died, and Sofia escaped back to her mother who was still begging at the gate.

"Who is it?" asked her mother.

"It's me, Sofia." Would her mother be angry? Did her mother hate her for leaving? She awaited her mother's response.

Finally, her mother embraced her little girl who was not little any longer.

"I have everything here that I needed," said Sofia through her tears. "I will never leave you again."

Treaz blinked back her own tears. She missed her old life and her Grammie terribly. Would she forgive her for being gone? As Treaz became older, she reasoned that her grandmother's fairy tales came from old Romanian folklore meant to teach children life lessons. How true that old tale of Sofia had now become.

No longer able to stop them, Treaz allowed her tears to flow. How inaccurate her read on people had been. Her assumptions meant nothing because she never took the time to ask anyone the truth about their lives. No wonder she was a loner.

After the water lost its heat, she stood and turned on the shower to wash her hair—another wonderful pleasure. She rubbed the entire bottle of lotion all over her body. It stung when it touched a spot on her Host's inner, upper arm that was red and probably infected. The half-inch long incision was in the same exact spot as on all her past Host bodies. That couldn't be a coincidence. It must mean something.

The new dress slipped over her cleansed body, and she admired herself in the mirror. Underneath all that grime, she—well, Zoe, appeared quite pretty, and her brown eyes seemed to have gained a sparkle. The library clerk and café hostess would grant her entrance for sure.

In the restaurant across the road, Treaz ordered an advertised special—a dinner salad with ranch dressing, a chicken with pasta entree, and a piece of chocolate cake for dessert. The server politely asked if she would like some wine. Even though it sounded enticing, just one glass, she thought of her promise to Richard, and declined. She consumed every last bite of her meal.

On the way back to the luxurious room that awaited her, her belly now full, Treaz approached a homeless woman sitting at the edge of the alley, her face dirty and clothes worn. Next to her were two paper sacks held all her worldly belongings. She may have been about forty, but it was hard to tell. The streets made people appear beyond their years.

The woman glanced up, not knowing anything about where Treaz had been over the last days. Treaz reached into her pocket and pulled out a twenty dollar bill and handed it to her.

"God bless you," the woman said, her eyes a bit brighter. She tucked the bill inside her shirt.

"No," replied Treaz. "God bless *you*."

At the hotel, Treaz crawled in between the fresh sheets and snuggled her head into the feather pillow. She needed to deal with things better; try to have a more positive attitude despite her circumstances. In the morning she would find her Asset, and get her assignment underway. She looked forward to meeting Richard at the library the day after tomorrow and finding out more about Vanguard.

30
OMANI

The next time Omani and Iggy messaged each other, he held her to the commitment of sharing her family story.

IM: K. Your turn to tell me about your parents.

OL: Well, the easy one is my father. I never knew him and have no memories. He left us before I turned a year old. Mom said probably because she worked too much.

IM: Parents do that sometimes. What about your mom?

Omani sighed. Where to begin? She shouldn't burden Iggy with too many details, yet she didn't want to sugar coat anything either.

OL: She was a general practice doctor. People adored her. She had a wonderful disposition...eager to help everyone. No one was ever turned away if they couldn't pay as Mom somehow found a way to make it work.

IM: She sounds amazing, but you're talking about her in the past tense...

OL: Yeah. She died a long time ago. I miss her.

IM: I'm sorry, O. What happened?

OL: She, her friend Julia, and I were planning a trip to the United States. I said something about it in front of my Uncle that triggered his ungodly temper—still don't know why he was so upset. He and my mom got into a huge argument.

IM: Gnarly.

OL: Then my mother got extremely ill and ended up dying.

IM: Did that all happen right away?

OL: Within a few weeks.

Omani waited for Iggy's delayed response.

IM: Um, was that kinda suspicious? I mean that happening right after their big fight.

She remembered being so broken by the loss of her mother, just dealing with the heartache left no room for wondering seriously about why it happened. It seemed unfathomable that Filip would cause the death of his own sister over some minor disagreement.

OL: I was just sixteen trying to cope. Then he became my legal guardian, and he moved into our house. He let people come over who just sat around drinking and smoking, and messing up everything then made me clean after them. I hated being there and started thinking perhaps my Uncle did have something to do with my mother's death. Yet, I never found any proof.

IM: Must've been awful.

Omani remembered standing up to her Uncle.

"Why does someone have to stay at school with me? It's embarrassing to have some strange man watching me all the time," Omani said.

Filip snapped at her. "You're my responsibility now, and I don't have time to take you myself."

Omani came closer to his desk. She'd already come up with a good solution. "I could live with Julia."

Filip shook his head vehemently. "Out of the question."

"Why not? She lives close—"

"We're moving soon. I'm going to hire someone to teach you privately."

Outraged, Omani shook her head. "But, I've got friends. I don't want to move!"

He tried to dismiss her with the wave of his arm.

She held her ground. "I think you did something to her."

He scowled. "What'd you say?"

Her fists clenched. "You made my mom sick and let her die."

Filip calmly rose to his feet, and came to stand six inches from her face. His ugly eyes burrowing into hers. "Your mother was a terrorist."

Omani's heart raced. Yet, she refused to look away, no matter how frightening it felt. "You're lying," she screamed.

"Did she explain everything she was doing?" he said coldly. "Did she keep locked drawers and computer passwords? Did she make you leave when she had conversations with people?"

Her eye's flooded with tears and her stare dropped to the floor. All those things were true. Her mother did secretive work with Julia. She kept a drawer locked in the bottom of her desk which held her Green Mystery Folder. But, no, her mother couldn't have been a part of anything horrible like terrorism, could she?

Filip put his hand on Omani's shoulder. "Your mother loved you. She just got caught up in the wrong things."

"How?" asked Omani, her voice shaking.

"She was helping bad people. Julia got her mixed up in it."

Omani's heart ached, and she couldn't or didn't want to wrap her head around the facts Uncle Filip claimed. What if he was telling the truth?

"The world is not a safe place for you. Please, you must trust me. Your life is in danger if certain people recognize you," he said.

OL: He made me move with him a few months later. I guess he came into some money or something with his new business, and that's when he built this Compound we live on. It's beautiful, but a prison. My prison. Everyone can leave except me, because of the threat against me.

IM: I can't imagine. You think that you're actually in danger?

Over the years, Omani had grown used to her lot in life. Honestly, she didn't know what was true and what wasn't. She did know that as a single mom, Hanna had kept them in a nice house in a good neighborhood, and always found time to attend Omani's school English and History presentations. She saved people's lives and healed sick people. She was extremely smart. Her mother had also instructed Omani to not say anything about Franklin to anyone, and aside from mentioning him by mistake to Filip, Omani had kept that promise. She would not break it, not even with Iggy.

OL: Maybe. I don't really know.

IM: Wish there was some way I could help.

How sweet of him. Then self-scolding hit quickly. Omani didn't want to get Iggy involved with anything. She tried to backtrack in case he was unknowingly employed by her Uncle's organization.

OL: I make it sound bad, but I do like my job. Things run smoothly because of me.
IM: No doubt. You seem to be a very smart woman.

She exhaled, not convinced she was worthy of his compliment. If she truly was so smart, shouldn't she have found a way out of her prison by now? Why had she just given up trying? Talking about her mother made her suddenly sad. She didn't feel like chatting any longer.

OL: I'd better go now, Iggy.
IM: Take care, O. Thanks for sharing your family stuff. Talk soon.

Omani crawled into bed, her thoughts returning to her last moments with her mother. She still saw every detail of the stark white walls of the hospital room, the long tubes of clear fluid, the small television playing old game shows with the volume muted. She smelled the sharp antiseptic within the warmth of the room, and heard the chirps and rhythmic beeps of medical monitors.

Omani sat by her mother's bedside holding her hand, tears streaming down her face.

Her mother licked cracked lips and whispered, every word an effort. "Ani. I love you more than anything on this earth."

Pulling her mother's hand to her lips, Omani kissed it. "Oh, Momma. Please don't go. Don't leave me here."

The woman used her index finger to touch her daughter's wet face. "We all have something to do, Ani. You must find your something." Her eyes lost focus and slowly closed.

Omani stood, clinging to her mother. "I love you. I love you!"

The heart monitor turned to a long steady tone, and a nurse in the room switched it off. Omani broke into sobs as she rested her head on her mother's now motionless chest.

The memory remained as vivid as if it happened yesterday. Omani wiped her eyes with her night gown and pulled the bed covers up. Had she found her something yet? She could invent things like excelling at her job, or treating her employees with compassion and respect, but even though those felt admirable, they were not her something.

31

OMANI

Omani emerged from the bathroom ready for work. She switched on her computer and immediately saw Iggy's message.

IM: Hey hey, O? You there?

Her heart sped a little hoping nothing bad had transpired. It was unusual for him to reach out in the morning—in fact, he never did. Omani called down to Fritter. "I'm going to be a few minutes late." Then she replied to her friend.

OL: Hello, yes. Is everything alright?
IM: Yuppers. Happy New Year. I just wanted to check in with you after our chat about your mom. Are you OK?

He cared about her. She had not experienced someone's genuine concern over her feelings for a very long time.

OL: Thank you. I'm doing fine. Nothing a good night of crying and shut-eye can't fix.

That was a lie—actually, more of a distraction. She sighed. Her whole life felt like a distraction.

IM: So you've really never been off your Compound since high school?

OL: Only one time.

IM: What happened?

OL: I sweet-talked my new tutor to take me on an outing.

Omani explained running away at seventeen just to be captured in the gelato shop. It was also the first time she mentioned needing to use crutches, and her Uncle's harsh punishment of refusing to allow the surgery to get them fixed.

IM: Holy moly. That sucks.

OL: My Uncle was not happy with me.

IM: Did he EVER let you get your legs fixed?

OL: No. No snowboarding for me.

IM: What a #*%@. You can fill in any word you like.

She typed a smiley face.

OL: After that, he hired armed guards to monitor the premises 24/7. He must have come into more money because he started to drive fancy sports cars and sometimes brought women home with him—although they were always gone by the next morning. Ick. I can't imagine any woman wanting to be around him, let alone sleep with him.

IM: LOL

OL: I asked him why he needed so much security, and he told me to protect us from the people who refused to work for their own money and wanted to steal ours. Also, to keep the terrorists away from me.

IM: You never tried to run away again?

OL: One other time when I was twenty.

IM: How'd that go?

OL: A complete joke. With my crutches, I obviously wasn't the fastest kid on the block.

IM: 😄

OL: My Uncle's men caught me before I got half-way down the driveway. Man, was Uncle Filip upset at being summoned at 4:30 in the morning to deal with me.

IM: Wardens don't like to miss their beauty sleep. Do you believe that bad people are still after you?

The years had dulled any real concerns about it. Yet, a nagging remained. What would happen if her Uncle's claims were true? Could her life be in danger if she left the Compound?

OL: He used to conveniently leave an article or two near my breakfast plate about some horrible terrorist attacks. When I didn't react, he stopped. Honestly, I don't pay much attention to him anymore and try to avoid him as much as possible. I got so sick and tired of him just talking and talking.

IM: Made you wanna bite your ear off?

Omani laughed aloud. She liked Iggy.

OL: You have such a way with words.

IM: A single laugh guaranteed every hour.

OL: More like every minute.

She looked at her watch, not wanting to go, yet becoming uncomfortably late for work.

OL: How are your dogs?

223

IM: All sleeping at my feet. It'll be a long night here with all the fire crackers.

She hadn't witnessed fireworks since childhood. How wonderful it would be to enjoy their explosions and bursting colors in the night sky again.

Omani and Iggy bid goodbye to each other, and she went to work.

All day she thought about her new online friend and her answers to his questions. Why had she been so afraid to run again? A seed took hold in her mind—one she hadn't allowed herself to nurture for a very long time. Omani would find a way to leave the Compound. Her planning and troubleshooting skills had developed over the years, along with her maturity, so surely she could find a way. She had convinced Rafael to set up things, and she hadn't been found out. No one outside would recognize her these days, even if they were still searching.

She wanted to meet Iggy in person. The thought triggered a warm sensation in her chest. Suddenly she stood straighter and lifted her chin, confident she would finally travel to America. Somehow. By some miracle, could Franklin still be alive? He would be much older. She knew about the park by his house in Arizona. Iggy would certainly allow her to stay on his couch for a few days, and help her travel to Phoenix to find Franklin—the only person she knew from the United States. Except Iggy, of course.

Omani would talk to Iggy about her idea the next time they chatted. She clenched and released her toes and fingers. She could do it this time. Maybe it would be her New Year's resolution—something she hadn't made since being a kid, but, things would be different now.

32
TREAZ

Treaz awoke groggy from a heavy sleep. Something pressed rhythmically on her chest and gave a low, contented purr. While in Danielle's body, Treaz had gained more affection for the furry felines. Zoe must have picked up a stray. She blinked to focus coming face-to-face with a white cat with beautiful, large green eyes. The metal medallion dangling around its neck read Princess.

"Hello, Princess." She tried to stroke the animal, but her arms would not budge. That was new. Could her body still be asleep? She tried again, but nothing. A slight pins and needles sensation tingled in both her legs, and she attempted to wiggle her toes, but neither leg would move.

Her heart thumped faster. "Oh my, God."

Princess stopped kneading and settled in on Treaz's stomach, her eyes closing as the end of her tail twitched back and forth.

Treaz was paralyzed. *Don't panic,* she commanded herself, but her breathing increased as if she'd just sprinted a mile.

Able to move her head, she realized the hotel room had transformed into an airy bedroom painted a bright blue. Daylight streamed in through the window. Across the room sat a wheelchair with safety straps, and a high-mounted joy stick. Her eyes watered, and she squeezed them shut to prevent tears from escaping. A few ran down the sides of her face tickling her skin.

Unable to scratch the itch sent her face into contortions. Treaz moved her head roughly back and forth on the pillow in frustration.

"What did I do in my life to deserve this?" she screamed causing Princess to shoot off the bed, dashing to the refuge of the closet. Crying made her nose drip. The tissue box on the bedside table was totally inaccessible. Treaz willed herself to settle down by taking in long, deep breaths and releasing them slowly. She laid there, numb everywhere, not only in her limbs.

"It's temporary," she said aloud. "For a little while, a little while. I can get through this." She had no choice because no one else was going to help. Pearl Man seemingly didn't care. Aren't good bosses supposed to ensure a positive work environment for their employees? Defend them against bad decisions by upper management?

Princess stalked back and jumped up. Her long, slender whiskers bobbled as her nose sniffed Treaz's face. Did the feline suspect her owner had been replaced with a stranger? The two locked eyes inches apart as they examined each other. With a scratchy tongue, Princess licked Treaz's wet cheek. The tiniest of tiny smiles appeared as Treaz soaked in the cat's compassion. It seemed to sense her loneliness—or at least enjoyed the taste of salty water.

The bang of a door and footsteps made it apparent that someone was coming. They both turned their heads to the bedroom entrance. Pearl Man showed carrying the traditional Vanguard box. He stopped in the doorway and gawked, his mouth opening slightly.

Princess hissed and bolted back to the closet.

Treaz held his gaze, not caring about the visible mess on her face. His jaw tightened.

Good. He needed to see her like this to experience a hint of what it was like to be a Transitioner.

After a moment, Pearl Man blinked, turned away, and walked across the room to place the small box on the dresser. "I knew you'd need me to begin this one," he said with a false cheeriness.

She nodded down at her body. "What the hell is this all about?"

"Good morning to you, too," he said opening the flaps on the box. "Let's find out, shall we?" He removed a small, leather wallet and opened it. "Your name is Elizabeth Sandoval, and you are…" His eyes raised to calculate the number, "thirty-seven years old."

She scoffed. Remembering her anger at being jerked from one body to another without closure regarding the previous life, Treaz blurted out, "You people don't care about your employees; they're just commodities."

He set the wallet down. "You're upset."

"Bingo," she said sarcastically. "Why do you people yank me around so much? I'm trying to do my job, but you don't even let me finish my assignment."

"Are you certain?"

Treaz wanted to throw her hands up, but nothing moved, leading to more frustration. "I never even found the Asset because I was so caught up with Zoe's troubles."

"Not so."

She frowned at him.

"Richard was likely your Asset."

"But, I didn't do anything for him. He's the one who helped me."

"And by doing so, you helped him. That fulfilled your assignment. You re-inspired him to move forward in his life with whatever it is he's meant to do."

"I promised to meet him at the library." She turned her head away and murmured. "It's not right."

He walked to the window and looked out.

"I'm worried about Zoe. Will she be okay?"

"She's back."

"Where was she when I was her?" Pearl Man did not answer. "If I have to do this damn job, why can't I do it from my own body and keep some semblance of a normal life? I mean, this seems a bit much. Why not hire me to do this without all this switching around? You do your job in your own body, right?"

He nodded and sighed. "They don't want you to carry on with your regular life but rather be immersed in your work."

She grimaced at the thought that she couldn't possibly be anymore immersed than being in Elizabeth's body.

"They need you in a different environment. One where the Host would be more naturally in contact with the Asset."

"We," Treaz said.

"What do you mean?"

"You keep saying *they* but you should be saying *we* since you're one of them."

Pearl Man shoved his hands in his pockets, looking to the floor.

"This job really sucks."

"I know," he agreed.

Princess poked her head from the closet door, scampered across the room, and up a carpeted tower in the corner. She crammed into a dark cubby hole finding refuge.

"Please can you just introduce me to someone I can be friends with?"

Pearl Man's harsh reaction startled her. "I said no before. No means no. Don't ask me again."

"What's your problem?" she matched his impassioned tone. "I'm the one with issues here."

Rubbing his face, he crossed the room, nodding.

He seemed more unsettled than she'd seen him before. Treaz softened her voice. "What's going on, Pearl Man?"

"Nothing. Sorry. Never mind."

"Seriously, you can trust me. Who am I going to tell?"

Pearl Man looked at her, contemplating. "Vanguard's pushing. There's a lot more pressure on everybody, right now."

"For what?"

"Having our Transitioners move more quickly. Getting them to be more efficient and effective at influencing people."

Treaz cocked her head. "Why?"

"Something big's coming, but nobody knows what it is."

"If you're so unhappy, why don't you just quit?"

"I tried doing that once and was told they don't let people leave. People are Displaced."

"What's that mean?"

Pearl Man shook his head.

"Will I ever get back to my life, or is that another lie Vanguard makes you tell us?"

"No. Transitioners do eventually return. They feel confident that if you speak about anything, you'll be diagnosed as mentally unstable. Not so easy with Counselors. You cannot mess with these people, Treaz." He consulted his watch. "I've got to go."

She didn't want him to go. Even though he annoyed her much of the time, someone was better than no one. "I've got a job for you before you leave," she said.

"What's that?"

"I need you to wipe my nose. The box is right next to me."

After a moment of hesitation, Pearl Man walked over, pulled out a tissue, and gently rubbed it around her nose. Then using a

229

second one, dabbed it across her cheeks. This was the first time he had actually touched her besides a hand on her shoulder. She could smell the faint scent of his soap or perhaps shampoo. Treaz watched his eyes although he kept his averted. "Look at me," she said softly. He kept his eyes focused on the tissue. Her voice grew louder, more stern. "I said, look at me."

Pearl Man connected, and they maintained an extended stare. She saw his eyes begin to glisten with tears as he bit his lip. Maybe the work pressure was having a bigger impact than he could handle and he was overdue for a vacation. Why would he be so emotional? A few times he'd apologized to her, and seemed to somewhat pretend to understand her exasperation with the various situations she'd been in. But his watery eyes communicated something deeper. She found herself feeling a little sorry for him. "Why are you crying?"

"You have eyes like your mother," he whispered.

She gasped. "What did you say?"

He backed away, dropping eye-contact. "I said you have eyes like my mother."

"No, you didn't. You said I had eyes like *my* mother."

"I have to go. Someone's coming soon to help you."

"That's not fair. I find this out and you're going to leave? I can't even get up out of this wretched bed and block the door." He stopped. Her mind raced. She badly wanted to shake him or slap him or stomp her feet. Her tears accumulated again as she imagined her mother's beautiful blue eyes. "So, Elizabeth's eyes are blue." He nodded. "Why didn't you tell me about my mother before?" No response. "Hang on. Was she a Transitioner, too?"

He paused and returned to her side. "Yes."

Treaz's mother had experienced this nightmare as well. All the waking up in stranger's bodies for the sake of Vanguard's whims. "When?"

230

"I was her Counselor when I first started, way before you were born. Vanguard seeks out people with specific genetic coding. Usually they skip generations, but in your case, your mother's effectiveness was so high, they decided to bend the rules. Against my strong recommendation."

"She was a worse loner than me."

"Being a loner doesn't preclude you from having influence on people," he said.

That was a statement Treaz had come to believe during her short time as a Transitioner.

"Rarely do they find the right combination of genes, but when they do, like in your family, results are as much as three times the success rate of the typical Transitioner. Only certain people have this advanced ability."

"What makes us so good?"

"I honestly don't understand it all."

"What about genes from my father?"

He shrugged.

"Does Vanguard know who he is?"

"No."

"How can you be so sure?"

"Because your mother had obviously already finished her Transitioning work when she got pregnant. And, because I know more about you than you think. I do my homework on all my Transitioners."

Treaz shook her head at him. "That's creepy. Really creepy. You're just a creepy guy, Pearl Man."

His eyebrows rose defensively. "I said I disagreed with them taking you in the first place."

"Why can't you let me go home? Say that I ran away, and you couldn't find me."

"Unfortunately, it's not how it works."

"How does it work, then?"

His tone changed back to the old Pearl Man, he moved away from her heading towards the door. "I already said too much."

"Wait. I have more questions."

"Of course you do."

"What am I supposed to do now without help?"

He exhaled loudly, considering the time again. "Someone will be here soon."

"Please, think about the friend thing," Treaz called out as he walked from the bedroom.

He glanced back, then disappeared. A moment later, the front door closed with a slam. Princess reemerged from the cubby hole and found her way back to Treaz's chest, nuzzling her face intimately. "How sad that I can't pet you." Yet, somehow she perceived that the cat accepted her inability to move and loved her anyway.

She stared up at the ceiling. Was there a reason she had been put in this strange, messed-up situation? Some lesson she was supposed to learn? Her mind filled with her experiences from the last two weeks. Treaz had certainly learned more about compassion—definitely something previously lacking in her life. Perhaps all this was happening to make her a better person?

Had her mother also endured assignments like Zoe or Elizabeth? No doubt she had. How long did she suffer in the Transitioner role? Had her experiences caused her mental illness? It surely must have had some effect. Did Grammie know? How could she not have known? If Treaz could only talk to her grandmother on the phone.

Treaz hoped she wouldn't end up like her mother—paranoid, afraid, and withdrawn. She must stay alert taking as much control over her circumstances as she could while residing in all the different bodies.

Forget all that positive thinking crap she planned during that last night in Zoe's world. Knowing that today would assuredly not be the last time she awoke in a stranger's body, Treaz vowed to do everything she could to be difficult. She would become one rebellious Transitioner, making Vanguard fire her even if Pearl Man got Displaced, whatever that meant. Treaz would fight her way home. No longer was she frightened, but empowered. However, first, she needed to get out of the restricted body she was currently in.

33

OMANI

Filip stood, red-faced. "Get rid of him, then. Find others who can do the work. Or do I need to replace you?"

Omani watched him talk on the phone, and she braced herself for his residual anger.

"Damn Counselors," he said, dropping his cell on the desk and plopping into his chair. "Practically impossible to hire dependable people."

A Counselor? There certainly were no employees on the Compound with the title Counselor. She'd have to investigate.

Omani wanted to enlighten Filip that people disliked being around him because he was such a tyrant but had learned from experience those opinions were best kept to herself. "You seem to be under a lot of pressure, Uncle Filip." He rubbed his forehead. "Perhaps you'd enjoy a nice vacation. You haven't taken one in years," she said, sincerely not caring. Him being gone would offer her a better chance of vanishing off the property without him finding out right away.

The slamming of his hand made her jump. "A vacation? There's no time for a vacation."

Omani raised her hands. "I thought maybe—"

"Just handle the new hires faster. Forget the tour and orientation or whatever you do with them. I need them working."

"They should understand—"

"Skip it," Filip said. His phone rang again.

Omani left his office not desiring to listen to his anger taken out on anyone else. She would still find a way to do the right thing. Everyone starting a new job deserved proper information and training.

When she found a way to leave, she would start her own business in America. Her efficiencies in running a large household might open some opportunities. She spent the day pondering in-between her daily job duties and handling her own employee challenges.

Late in the afternoon, Omani was summoned to the Researchers' office. Omani listened patiently to a disgruntled employee's complaints about the choice of new office chairs.

"My lower back hurts after sitting in it for ten minutes," exaggerated the unhappy man.

Omani apologized and told him she would order him another one. That somewhat appeased him. He offered an understated thanks, gathered his things, and left her alone in the office.

She began to exit, then stopped. Being in that work area, with no Researchers was unusual. Perhaps she should…

The door opened and another Researcher entered, surprised to see Omani standing there.

Think quick!

"Hi," began Omani. "I'm so glad I caught someone. Filip asked if I'd stop by and pick up the latest list of Counselors."

The man frowned. "You?"

Omani shrugged. "I don't know. He just said it was important."

He stood for a few moments, then nodded and went to his computer. "I'll send it—"

"Oh," she exclaimed. "He said he wants a paper copy."

The man turned back to her. "Really?"

"Is that a problem? He seemed kind of in a hurry."

"It's going to take some time to print out."

Omani gave a friendly smile. "I can wait."

He exhaled and entered some keystrokes. "Okay, I'll get it started." Once the printer began to run, he picked up his apparently forgotten cell phone and left.

She stood watching the papers spit out of the printer. After five pages, the machine jammed. "No," she said aloud and tried to unsuccessfully clear the problem. Footsteps passed by the office door causing a stab in her stomach. She couldn't get caught with any papers! Quickly she scooped up what had printed, shoved them in her sling, and made her way out of the door. Two other Researchers passed her in the hallway avoiding any eye-contact.

34

OMANI

After the dinner hour and back in her living quarters, Omani dropped the printed papers from the Researchers' office on her desk. She could look them over later. Messaging Iggy was foremost in her mind as she was anxious to tell him her plans to leave the Compound. Well, not complete plans yet, but the idea of escaping.

OL: Hello, Iggy.
IM: O! Whatcha up to in marvelous chilly Swizzy-land?

She laughed aloud liking his lightheartedness.

OL: Just finished work. How about you in the old U.S. of A?
IM: Weather's fantastic. Dogs are great. Chatting to my favorite person.

Was he flirting with her? She shook her head and smiled. Though he likely was on the younger side, it still felt pleasant for someone to be interested.

OL: I enjoy chatting with you as well.

IM: We start with the most important topic of the evening, or morning in my case.

She cupped her face in her hands. He's excited to tell her something as well.

OL: What's that?
IM: Guess whose birthday's today? I'm an archaic twenty-six years old!

Omani gasped, then chuckled. Younger, but she had not guessed by that much.

OL: A baby. Happy birthday!
IM: Thanks. Wish we could grab a drink. It'd be cool to hang out in person sometime.
OL: That would be fun.
IM: Can you really not leave your home?

She flexed her fingers, dying to bring up her idea and ask for his help in developing her plan for freedom.

OL: Not yet.
IM: I'll come see you if I can find someone to watch the pooches. Bet I could find a sweet deal on Kayak.
OL: ???
IM: You never heard of Kayak?
OL: I don't get out. Remember?
IM: LOL. Of course. It's a travel website.

She refrained from mentioning the futility of Iggy trying to visit the Compound. No way Uncle Filip would grant him passage through the front gate.

IM: When's your birthday, O?

No one ever bothered to ask anymore, but Iggy did. She bit her lip.

OL: I was born on September 11th. A horrible day in your country.
IM: It was. Perfectly burned in everybody's mind.
OL: My YDI puts me at thirty-five.

There came a pause before Iggy's reply.

IM: What do you mean YDI?
OL: Youth Device Implant. What do you call them in America?
IM: Uh. I have no idea what that is.

Omani frowned. How can a country as advanced as the United States not use YDI's?

OL: A little round disc they put in the back of your neck to make you look and feel more youthful. You must have heard of them.
IM: Is it like an experimental thing?
OL: I've had mine for ten years. My Uncle's had his for over twenty. Most people get them when they hit fifty.
IM: I'm pretty tech savvy. I'm trying to understand why I'm not aware of such technology. How old are you, really?

For the first time, his questions lost their charm. Why did her age matter? Had he truly thought they would ever be more than friends? She didn't want to answer. When he repeated his question, she sighed.

OL: Turning sixty this year.
IM: Wait. What?
OL: My birthday was September 11th, 2001.
IM: Like THE September 11th, 2001?

Was he rubbing it in her face?

OL: What other one is there?

Another extended delay. She grimaced. He probably thought she was inappropriate for messaging him since she was technically old enough to be his grandmother.

IM: Is this some kind of joke?

A joke? Why would he ask that?

OL: Absolutely not.
IM: Did you hit your head or something?
OL: Why are you being this way, Iggy? I promise, I'm telling you the truth. Sorry I didn't tell you my biological age before, but I honestly didn't think it was a big deal. People with YDI's live as their younger selves and that makes me thirty-five. That's not like—
IM: You need to explain something to me.
OL: Of course.

IM: If you were born in 2001, that'd make you only sixteen.

Omani rolled her desk chair back and stared at his last statement. "If you were born in 2001, that'd make you only sixteen."

The words of his next message flashed across the screen.

IM: You're insinuating it is 2061. Really? You're sticking with that story?
OL: It is 2061.
IM: Forty-four years in the future. I'm not into your practical joke.

She was so confused.

OL: No, I swear. What year is it there?
IM: Seriously? Like being in a different country means anything?
OL: Please, just tell me. What year?

After a few moments, Iggy finally replied.

IM: 2017.

That can't be right. Jumping up, she grabbed her crutches and paced back and forth across the room. Her heart pounded. How was that possible? How?

Iggy had a good sense of humor, but this did not seem like something he would think was funny. In fact, she sensed a touch of irritation in his messages. There was no way either one of them could prove there was a forty-four year difference between them. He couldn't tell her anything that happened in the future and anything she shared about the past, he wouldn't know about yet.

Omani went into her bathroom and stared at herself in the mirror. Who could she ask to help figure this out? No one. If only her mother was there, she would help Omani understand… wait. She pinched her cheeks. Could her mother have had something to do with this? She was the only person that would have been genius enough to figure out how to communicate with the past.

Oh God. She ran a hand through her hair.

Had Franklin been in the past as well? She recalled the excitement in her mother on that first night when he contacted her. But how she had delayed responding until Omani was in school.

She recollected her mother's evasive reactions sometimes, like her insisting on checking with Franklin first before Omani could interact with him. Him fabricating the lame excuse that his wife wouldn't allow him to meet them on their trip to America. And Omani's gift. Even when she insisted on leaving his birthday gift in the park near Franklin's home, his instructions were she'd better package it up well. No wonder her mother wanted to see what was going into the box, so she could covertly inform Franklin. That would allow him to provide the appropriate thank you to Omani despite him never receiving the gift at all. It made sense now. If it actually had ever been delivered, Franklin wouldn't be picking it up until later that year, in 2017.

At times in her chats with Franklin, she chalked up his cryptic messages to him being a typical adult who couldn't relate to teenagers. But now she understood the real reason why.

A sense of relief fell over her and she let her head fall back as she stared at her ceiling. Her mom wasn't planning for terrorist attacks. The only thing she probably conspired about was to keep private the knowledge of her and Franklin's time difference.

She sucked in and released a long breath and went to look out her window at the twinkling stars. It was the same sky she looked out at for almost six decades. Grasping her pewter ladybug necklace in her hand, she shut her eyes. "Oh, Momma," she whispered. "Why didn't you tell me?"

This called for something sugar-packed. She retrieved her carton of gelato from her hidden freezer. Omani didn't bother utilizing a bowl, she simply scooped out over-sized spoonfuls. No time for savoring.

Everything had changed that night Omani accidentally brought up in front of Uncle Filip her and her mother's planned vacation to America; although never, until the current moment, had she been so certain that Filip had murdered his own sister. The reason for the fatal outcome after that deadly argument was now evident. Once he found out her mom was in touch with someone from the past, he wanted in. So he eliminated who was in the way, took all her work, and got wealthy from her untimely death.

How was Filip making his fortune? That would be something she needed to expose. She thought about her mother's last words, "Ani, you must find your thing." Maybe Omani's thing was putting a stop to Filip and avenging the death of Hanna LaZarres, her beautiful mother.

Chewing on a frozen chunk of strawberry, she wrestled with why Filip hadn't made her fatally ill like he had her mother. Perhaps he originally feared it would appear too suspicious and was afraid he might get caught. Nowadays, he held Omani hostage probably because she worked like a dog, for free. No wonder Filip imprisoned her on the Compound, keeping her technology access to a minimum. Even Rafael commented recently about her electronic pad being ancient. "Something for a museum," he had said.

How she despised Uncle Filip.

The overload of sugar created some stomach upset, and she put what little gelato that was left away.

If only she had been able to get her hands on her mother's green folder before Filip stole it. It must have been bursting with details and facts. She removed her own Green Mystery Folder and flipped through the few contents collected over the years. Perhaps something fresh would emerge amongst the once meaningless pages. Old receipts found behind file cabinets with ink were now too faded to read any longer. The uninformative, short obituary on her mother's death obtained through the fired Researcher made her hunger for more information. The most recent half shredded printout about the college student who had been kicked out of school years before left her wondering. Still, no answers there. At least not yet.

Closing the slim file, she felt more empowered to find a way to escape and go to the United States. Iggy would be seventy, and might even already be dead. Poor guy. No surprise he was questioning her. It wasn't his fault. He was presumably just as mystified.

How could she convince him that she was telling the truth?

A thought jammed into her head like a bullet, and she held her breath. Wait. If her mother made the connection through the same means, whatever that was, might Iggy have known Franklin?

She rushed back to her computer.

OL: Iggy?

His comeback came swiftly.

IM: Yeah. Just been sitting here punching numbers in my calculator app. I think you've been locked up on your Compound too long.

OL: I do not have the slightest idea of how this is possible, but I think maybe it has something to do with my mother's work. I've got a question for you.

IM: Just one?

OL: Did you know someone named Franklin Mann?

IM: Um. That was my dad's name.

It was true! Iggy not only knew Franklin, but was his son. She grasped the sides of her head as an unexpected giggle emerged. Everything was becoming weirdly comical.

OL: Iggy, I knew your father.

IM: What? I never told you his—

OL: When he was thirty-one.

IM: No way.

OL: He lived in Phoenix, Arizona. There was a large park about a mile from his house. He worked from home and was married at the time with a pregnant wife.

Iggy didn't respond. She pressed fists against her chin.

OL: I didn't meet him in person, but on the computer.

IM: I'm still in that house and take the dogs to the park every morning. That must have been my half sister. Holy moly, O. Why didn't you say so?

She smiled and exhaled. *There* was her Iggy.

OL: Because I didn't realize you were his son.

IM: This is getting kinda bizarre.

OL: Your father never mentioned me, did he? He knew me as Omani. Nobody calls me O, except for you.

IM: Nay a word. You think he was up on this whole time thing?

OL: I'm betting both he and my mother knew and decided not to tell me. No doubt my mom figured I'd have blabbed about it to my friends.

IM: Well, good old Pops never told me anything, either. This is one hell of a breakthrough.

Omani widened her eyes and exhaled. What an understatement. Then her throat tightened. In January 2017, her mother would still be living. Why hadn't she thought of this before?

OL: Iggy, my mother is still alive in 2017, at least right now. She didn't die until later in the year.

IM: Wow. Nutty. Wait. Didn't you say your Uncle had something to do with her death?

OL: Yes.

IM: Then, if I could find her, I could warn her about what's going to happen.

Omani squeezed her hands. Might that work? Would her mother believe a stranger from another country who got in touch with her out of the blue? Of course, Iggy could explain he's Franklin's future son, but her mother didn't even know Franklin yet. Everything was moving so quickly.

OL: I love the idea, but let's think about things first. In your time, Uncle Filip still hasn't found out about your dad. In fact, our parents haven't met...well, communicated. We should wait until that happens.

IM: Makes sense. How much time do we have?

OL: Several months. Maybe six. There's so much to talk about. So, so much.

IM: Yeah. This boat load of curiosity is sinking my ship.

Her own interest now piqued as to what she had missed in the news over the past forty-four years. She massaged her temples attempting to stop a headache from breaking in.

OL: This is a lot to process. Let's chat tomorrow.

IM: What? But I got like a bazillion questions! 😳

OL: I do too.

IM: You got all the answers.

No, she didn't. Not yet, at least.

OL: Isn't that against the rules?

IM: Rules? You mean telling me what happens in the future?

OL: Yes. That was in a fantasy book I read one time. Couldn't there be an effect on things?

IM: Ah. The old time-travel conundrum. If you went back in time, could you influence the future? We aren't traveling, only messaging.

Omani shook her head. She needed time to think.

OL: I hear you, but I'm feeling sort of overwhelmed right now.

IM: Alright. I can dig that.

OL: I'll message you soon, OK?

IM: Right on. We'll resolve all the problems in the universe then.

OL: Thanks for not thinking I'm a nut-case.

IM: The jury's still noodling that one. 🙂 Goodnight O, from the future.

He got one last smile out of her.

OL: Night Iggy, from the past.

Her head spun with the unknown, yet deep down a sense of adventure bubbled. She was so glad she hadn't just continued on with her boring, predictable life. Her desire to make a friend was winding up to be quite remarkable.

Omani vowed she would do something. Piecing things together was a decent first step. Next she would find a way to leave the Compound and her Uncle Filip forever. Convinced she could finally take back control of her own life, she couldn't remove the smile from her face. After so many years, Omani would be free.

The papers from the Researchers' office caught her attention and she picked them up. Although hoping for more revealing information, there wasn't more than names in bold with several other names underneath. Maybe they were Counselors along with their current patients. The names meant nothing. She paused on one name she'd never heard before.—Treaz. That was a pretty name.

Omani set the list down. It didn't tell her anything, but she did intend on learning something more that night. She would research all the major historical events happening since 2017. Since little sleep would happen anyway, she might as well start catching up with the world.

Follow along with our continuing story in the second book in the *Awake As A Stranger* trilogy. Here's a taste of *Rebellion*'s beginning for both Omani and Treaz.

1

OMANI

Omani fumbled to turn off her 5:00 am alarm. Her eyes slowly blinked open and she stared at the ceiling. *Iggy's father is my old friend Franklin. Unbelievable!* She smiled.

Her mind replayed the revelations—how brilliant her mother had been, that Omani had somehow re-kindled her mother's original connection, and the forty-four year time difference existing between Iggy, her new online friend, and their worlds. She struggled trying to comprehend such an incredible possibility.

Most of her night had been spent on internet research about historical events occurring over the past four decades. Although Omani wanted to share her excitement about her discoveries with…well, someone, her secret must remain. Besides, she had to get to an early-morning meeting. She placed her crutches under her arms and dragged herself to the shower.

Uncle Filip had finally agreed to Omani's plans to remodel the Compound kitchen. Normally she would enjoy the process of picking out colors, counter tops, cabinets, and appliances, but it held no real thrill compared to what her and Iggy had uncovered through their messaging the night before.

After the exhaustive contractor meeting, and a quick dinner, Omani carried a cup of coffee to her living unit. A dose of caffeine would help extend her day a bit longer, so she could message Iggy for a while. Omani sent him a greeting. He began with an apology.

IM: I hope I didn't offend you by suggesting we go for a drink.

OL: Were you trying to pick me up?

IM: 😶 Sorry. I just had no clue you were older.

OL: It's fine. I never told you my age. Actually, I was quite flattered.

IM: Still friends?

OL: Friends.

IM: Cool beans.

A smile spread across her face. Iggy—the master of old clichés and the invention of new ones. He did have some strange vernacular. Must be an American thing.

OL: I'd been planning on telling you something before we got side-tracked last time.

IM: I did kinda upset the apple cart.

OL: I've decided I want to try to leave again.

IM: You mean escape the Compound?

OL: Yes and come to America.

IM: Yeah. You can't stay there now. Especially knowing what your crazed Uncle has kept buried all these years.

Her jaw clenched. The resentment towards Filip always bubbled just below the surface and sometimes flared to anger, but never had her hatred for him been so overwhelming, believing he now had had something to do with her mother's death. Staying on the Compound—her prison, seemed unbearable, but leaving to enter a world Omani didn't understand much frightened her.

OL: I'm not sure that's a brilliant idea anymore. I don't know anyone in the U.S.

IM: You know me.

OL: But, you'd be seventy now.

IM: See! We'd be a couple old-timers and COULD have a legit date!

She burst into laughter.

OL: Still trying, huh?

IM: Never say never. 😵

OL: You're very funny.

IM: This definitely is one of those mind-bending time travel stories.

OL: Except, I wouldn't literally be traveling back in time. It would be present day America in 2061.

IM: Do you think everybody working for your Uncle knows about this time thing?

Could everyone have kept such a considerable secret from her for all these years? Likely her direct staff wouldn't be trusted with those details. It was difficult to believe every one of her Uncle's employees knew, and nothing had leaked out.

OL: Probably only a few people.

IM: Did you tell anyone?

OL: Absolutely not.

IM: Not even that guy who set up your internet access?

OL: I don't think Rafael knows or he certainly would have hinted about it.

IM: And he's trustworthy?

OL: If not, I would have been called out on things by now. I've been reading about terrorism over the past forty years. For the known cases that have been stopped, my Uncle's organization is never mentioned.

IM: What do you think he's doing then?

OL: All I can tell is they do a bunch of computer research. We have lots of Researchers on staff.

Omani chewed her lip. Trusting Iggy was easy. Never had she doubted who he claimed to be because he had always come across as honest and sincere; just a really nice guy which made it extra hard to broach her suspicion. As she fondled the insulated metal mug, admiring the large red letter "V" on its side, she declared her fears.

OL: I think you're working for my Uncle.

IM: No frickin' way would I work for such a jerk face.

OL: You employed by Vanguard?

IM: Well dang. That's who I get my direct deposit paychecks from.

Closing her eyes, she exhaled deeply with the weight of the truth…

2

TREAZ

After Pearl Man, her unpredictable boss and Counselor, had left the apartment belonging to her latest Host body, Treaz heard the front door open again, and footsteps came to her room. A burly, olive-skinned man, with a neatly trimmed black beard flecked with gray, around forty, entered the bedroom. Princess arched her back and hissed.

"Nice kitty," he said in a Middle-Eastern accent.

Good kitty. Treaz prayed he was not the caregiver, perhaps a landlord or something. Her vulnerability in this stranger's body felt suffocating as she lay unable to move any of her limbs.

He walked to the bed. "Hello, Miss Sandoval. A pleasure to see you again."

Should she play dumb or play along? Treaz frowned.

He noticed. "You don't remember me?"

"Sorry."

"Daniel. I filled in for a day for Margaret several years ago."

Margaret must be her Host's regular caregiver. "You do look a little familiar," she lied. "Where is she?"

"Got a call this morning. She had to take emergency leave. Her sister was in a bad car accident in Florida."

Treaz figured this was another Vanguard move. That's how her employer worked, behind-the-scenes when no one paid attention. "When is she coming back?"

"I do not know. I just go where they send me."

Yeah, me too.

He walked over and reached for the blanket. "How about we get started?"

"Could you possibly make me some coffee?" she blurted out.

"Sure. How do you like it, Miss Sandoval?"

She'd rather go by Treaz, but, in her particular predicament, she opted to go by the Host's real name. "Elizabeth is fine. Just black."

Daniel left. She wanted to learn more about him before he saw her, or rather Elizabeth, nude. Soon the strong smell of coffee floated in from the kitchen. Returning with two cups, he raised the head of her bed and gave her a sip from one of them. It tasted bold and perfect.

"I'm sorry, what was your name, again?" Treaz asked.

He sat in a bedside chair. "Daniel."

She accepted another drink, rolling it around in her mouth. "I love the flavor." More accurately, she longed to prolong the *getting started* part. "How long have you been a caregiver?"

"Almost fourteen years. Too long."

"You don't like your job?"

Princess hopped on the bed. Daniel stood and moved her off. "I'm ready to do something different."

"I totally relate to that sentiment."

He folded his arms. "You don't like writing?"

Helpful information. Elizabeth must be a writer. Of course, she wasn't referring to her Host's line of work, and tried to cover

258

for her misdirected comment. "I mean, it's always fun to try new things. What do you want to do?"

Daniel looked upward, hesitating. Then offered a matter-of-fact response. "Expose the effects of radiation from electronic devices, and find an improved design."

Yes—he certainly is her Asset. "Wow. Very specific."

"I have been thinking about it for a long while now." He reached for the covers. "Alright, let's get you up."

No, no, no. "Can we wait a little longer? I'd like to relax a bit."

He bit his lip, and exhaled. "I'll begin cleaning, then."

The vacuum started up in the other room. Why couldn't Vanguard have given her a female Asset this time? Surely, Elizabeth's regular caregiver had *something* she hoped to accomplish. After about twenty minutes, he returned. "Ready now?"

"I don't think—"

"Look, Miss Sando—" Treaz tilted her head. "I mean, Elizabeth, I have to insist," he said. "I know you don't remember me—"

"Uh, and you *are* a man."

He exhaled. "I have seen hundreds of women's bodies. All ages. All shapes and sizes. This is part of my job."

Ugh. She'd just need to tell herself that he's looking at another woman's body, not hers. She sighed.

Daniel pulled back the sheet and blanket with a quick swoosh. "You always sleep naked?"

Her face flushed. This was so beyond the call of duty…

If you enjoyed *Awake As A Stranger - Awakening* please consider reviewing or rating it on Amazon, Goodreads, or other favorite sites. This really helps us independent authors by letting others know that the book is worth reading.

Thank you!

ABOUT THE AUTHOR

Diane has long been a lover of storytelling. She began her path down the world of sharing her stories in novels upon an unexpected move from Phoenix to Texas for 6 years. Now settled back in Phoenix, she continues to write. Diane also is passionate about independent filmmaking that offers her the opportunity to share her stories on film. She has written, directed and/or produced a feature film and several short films winning numerous awards for her efforts including receiving the 2012 Arizona Filmmaker of the Year Award.

Diane spent 27 years in corporate Human Resources and Training with most of that time in management and executive level positions in the financial and travel industries. She holds a Master's degree in Adult Education and a Bachelor's degree in Human Services.

Author & Blog Website: www.dianedresback.com
Filmmaking Website: www.mindclover.com
Facebook: dianedresback.author

A Note from Diane:

Thank you for going on the Awake As A Stranger journey! I would love to hear from you, so feel free to be in touch! I would be honored to have you in my readers email group which allows me to let you know when I have news or new books and importantly giveaways and discounts. You can sign up at either one of my websites: www.dianedresback.com or www.mindclover.com.

PUBLISHED PROJECTS

Awake As A Stranger: trilogy (fiction)
...Awake As A Stranger: Awakening
...Awake As A Stranger:: Rebellion
...Awake As A Stranger:: Altercation

From Us For You: Inspiring Stories of Healing, Growth and Transformation (non-fiction, compilation of 25 authors with net-proceeds of book sales donated to a nonprofit foundation assisting women)

Room For Another (fiction, based on true events)

Postponement (fiction)

Reminisce (fiction)

Promise of Protection (fiction)

Your Action, Your Success: Motivating Yourself to Get Things Done (non-fiction)

Elected Leader, Now What? (online course for leaders of volunteer groups available on teachable.com)